ECHO IN THE HALL:
DIVINE INTERVENTION

By Cricket Starr

Echo in the Hall: Divine Intervention
An Ellora's Cave Publication, December 2004

Ellora's Cave Publishing, Inc.
1337 Commerse Drive
Stow, Ohio 44224

ISBN #1-4199-5099-1

Other available formats: Microsoft Reader (LIT), Adobe (PDF),
Rocketbook (RB), Mobipocket (PRC) & HTML

This book is a work of fiction and any resemblance to persons,
living or dead, or places, events or locales is purely coincidental.
They are productions of the authors' imagination and used
fictitiously.

Edited by *Raelene Gorlinsky*
Cover art by *Syneca*

Warning:

The following material contains graphic sexual content meant for mature readers. *Echo In The Hall* has been rated *S-ensuous* by a minimum of three independent reviewers.

Ellora's Cave Publishing offers three levels of Romantica™ reading entertainment: S (S-ensuous), E (E-rotic), and X (X-treme).

S-ensuous love scenes are explicit and leave nothing to the imagination.

E-rotic love scenes are explicit, leave nothing to the imagination, and are high in volume per the overall word count. In addition, some E-rated titles might contain fantasy material that some readers find objectionable, such as bondage, submission, same sex encounters, forced seductions, etc. E-rated titles are the most graphic titles we carry; it is common, for instance, for an author to use words such as "fucking", "cock", "pussy", etc., within their work of literature.

X-treme titles differ from E-rated titles only in plot premise and storyline execution. Unlike E-rated titles, stories designated with the letter X tend to contain controversial subject matter not for the faint of heart.

Also by Cricket Starr:

Divine Interventions: Violet Among the Roses
The Doll

ECHO IN THE HALL
DIVINE INTERVENTIONS

By Cricket Starr

Chapter One

She came alive at midnight.

Alex crept down the darkened museum hallway and ducked behind one of the tall Grecian urns that flanked the opening to the adjacent gallery. From his hiding place he peered at the statue standing in the middle of the gallery. It was a beautiful thing, a slender stone figure of a woman just visible behind the marble representation of a tree. At the foot of the tree was a plaque: *Echo, A Greek Nymph*.

The face of the statue was frozen into a visage of longing and unrequited desire so poignant that when he'd first seen it, he'd thought her face the most beautiful in the world.

At least that's what he'd thought until several weeks ago when he worked late on a Thursday night and inadvertently discovered her true beauty.

The change in the statue started just as he heard the great clock in the museum lobby begin to chime twelve. At first it was subtle, just a hint of color to the white marble of the nymph's body, but then the color darkened and spread across the stone as if a film had been laid over it. Long curls of hair decorating her head and draping down her back darkened to pale gold, while rosy hues made pink her fingers and bare toes. A deep blush stole across the statue's cheeks as her lips deepened to the most enticing red.

For an instant the statue seemed alive as her eyelids blinked over irises now green instead of white, but then the film of color lifted away from the stone to form a ghostly outline of a woman, misty and indistinct. The ghost stepped back, leaving the statue as it had been—cold, unliving stone. As Alex watched, her transparency disappeared and she grew more solid, a spirit made beautiful flesh.

The first time he'd seen her come alive, he'd panicked, convinced he was seeing a ghost. Only the fact that he didn't carry a weapon had kept him from pumping lead into her—or more likely through her and into the museum wall. Thank goodness he hadn't done something that stupid. He'd certainly have had a problem explaining that to the museum's manager.

Without a gun, he'd remained frozen in place behind the stone urns until the ethereal figure had returned to the gallery to meld back into the statue, leaving no sign that she'd been there at all. When she'd repeated the process the following week, Alex had summoned the courage to follow her, this time noticing how tentative her movements were and how careful she was to avoid notice. She was more afraid than he was.

Alex grinned to himself. He'd found out what was pulling her out of her hiding place, why she was coming alive. By the third week, he was looking forward to her visit, watching her every move with fascination. Guarding an empty museum was usually pretty boring. With Echo coming to life, things had gotten more interesting.

This was the fourth week and he'd decided it was time for them to meet.

Alex wished he had his camera with him so he could capture her beauty for all time. Echo would make a marvelous model, he'd stake his growing reputation as a student photographer on it. As her body solidified, the simple white, off-the-shoulder gown she wore stayed sheer, revealing rose-tipped nipples and the inviting thatch of golden curls that covered her woman's mound.

Alex's cock hardened at the same time she did, and for once he was grateful for the looseness of his secondhand security guard's uniform. The job was temporary so rather than spend the money for a new one he'd made do with a castoff from the previous guard, a much larger man.

Pants that fit well would be very uncomfortable in his aroused state. Even so, it was hard not to groan aloud when she stretched her hands over her head and those heavy breasts lifted into full relief against their fabric covering.

Echo swung about in his direction, her dangly earrings making a soft tinkling in the quiet of the museum. Alex wondered if he'd made a noise, and froze in place, holding his breath. If she heard him, she'd flee back into the statue and he'd miss his chance tonight. She only came out on Thursdays at midnight, and even then only for this one specific purpose. Alex bit down on his lip.

Her great green eyes searched the darkness of the gallery, tension in her stance. For a moment Alex thought she would give up and flee, but then a woman's throaty laugh came from another part of the museum. Echo turned in that direction and longing replaced her watchful caution. She took a few hesitant steps then sped down the corridor in the direction the laugh had come from.

Moving as quietly as he could, Alex followed.

When he caught up with her, she was outside the entrance to the museum offices, her ear against the closed door. Alex heard another laugh, deep and male. Echo straightened and waved her hand and the door before her wavered, then appeared to fade away. Inside the now-revealed room, the occupants continued to talk and laugh, apparently unaware that they were exposed to Echo's rapt stare.

Alex took up a position behind the large urn across the hall. From his vantage point he could watch her and the couple inside the room.

"Nick, we've got to stop meeting like this." The museum's assistant curator, Violet Smith Rockman, ran her hand down the shirtfront of the tall handsome man standing next to her. "Someone's going to hear us."

Nicholas Rockman, associate professor of antiquities at the nearby city college, collected her hand and kissed it. "Since our daughter was born, the museum is the one place we can make as much noise as we want. You work late on Thursday night…this is the only time we do this, when no one is around."

Violet used her free hand to tug Nick's shirt out of his pants. "But the security guard…"

"…is way on the other side of the building." Nick slipped his hands under Violet's sweater, fondling the heavy breasts underneath. "We have twenty minutes before he gets back here."

"Twenty minutes…that's not much time." Violet's busy fingers sped along the buttons of Nick's shirt, revealing his lightly haired chest. She leaned over and licked his nipples, and Nick let loose a low groan.

Near the door, Echo put her hand over her mouth, suppressing her own groan.

"I know, but we still have enough time for this." Nick pulled Violet's sweater off and unfastened her bra.

As fascinated he was with Echo, Alex couldn't help but admire Violet's naked breasts. He knew she was breastfeeding but even so, they were enormous. Envy slashed through him as Nick kneaded the luscious globes and licked her swollen nipples.

Alex did his best to suppress a groan. He loved the feel of a plump nipple between his lips. One problem with his self-imposed celibacy was not having a woman's tits to suck.

Not that he'd really had a choice after Mel-the-Bitch had dumped him. His former girlfriend had taken exception to his leaving the lucrative business of marketing and applying to graduate school to study photography. Melody had been fine with his obsession of taking photos in his spare time, in the limited moments of the evening and the occasional weekend hours. She'd been too busy with her own concerns, spending time with her friends, trips to the shopping mall, manicures, and visits to the local spa.

Melody Martin had had any number of ways to spend her time — and his money — in entertaining herself.

But then he'd given up his soul-sucking job and announced that he was going back to school to study photography full time. It was his dream to become a professional photographer. The local university had classes he could take, but they were only offered during the day. He'd taken the security job at the museum to cover basic expenses so they'd have to scrimp for a while.

Once through school he could become a professional and earn a healthy income from doing what he loved best.

It would only take a little time, he'd told Mel.

Too much time, apparently. Melody had taken a single day to try and "talk sense" to him, and when she'd failed to change his mind had packed her bags and much of their apartment and left, cleaning out their joint bank account at the same time. She'd even taken the kitchenware they'd picked out and he'd paid for, leaving his cupboards as empty as his bed.

Alex grimaced over that. He could forgive the money, but eating on cheap plastic plates with mismatched silverware got to a man. He'd gained ten pounds in the past year, a tribute to a steady diet of pizza and other fast food washed down with too much beer. Mel's defection had left him with little appetite for anything else, including women of any kind.

Celibacy was easier than dealing someone who would cut your heart out when you were least expecting it, even if you had to give up sucking on plump nipples for a while.

Until he'd seen Echo he'd been relatively content with that situation. Now he watched her and desire sped through him, reminding him how nice being with a woman could be. Tonight he'd at least try for a taste of what he'd been missing.

By the door, Echo's eyes darkened with passion as she watched the couple making love. When Nick licked Violet's nipples, Echo licked her own fingers and ran them around her areolas, the circles dark through her flimsy gown. Her nipples grew hard and prominent through the thin fabric.

Alex smiled, imagining sucking on those luscious bits of her. *Soon, soon*, he promised himself.

In the office Violet tugged open Nick's belt and unfastened his pants. Nick's cock sprang out, fully erect. She went to her knees in front of him and licked the head, then drew the whole thing into her mouth. Nick's eyes closed and his head fell back, his breath deepening, matching time to Violet's movements.

Outside the doorway, Echo stared and she put her fingers into her mouth, attempting to mimic what Violet was doing to Nick. Alex's smile widened at her efforts. She was getting pretty good at it. He couldn't wait to test out her expertise on his own cock.

Speaking of which…watching the couple and the spying nymph was making his penis ache for attention.

Well, what would be the harm? As quietly as he could, Alex unfastened his pants and slid his erection out. He stroked himself with a far too practiced hand. It felt good, but not nearly what he knew Nick was feeling. Self-reliance had its limits. If only he could convince a handy mythical nymph to give him pleasure.

The mythical nymph in question had transferred her moistened fingers to the cleft between her legs, clutching her gown with her spare hand to get it out of the way. She worked her fingertips up and down her woman's folds, lingering in the sensitive spots. To Alex it looked like she was as practiced with this kind of self-pleasure as he was…and as frustrated by it.

Well, he had a fix for that, something he would propose just as soon Nick and Violet finished their little session, when Echo would head back to her statue. He had a plan that would leave both of them satisfied.

In the room, Violet's skirt came off and Nick slid her underpants down her thighs, past the stockings and garter belt she still wore. Stockings and a garter belt…Alex grinned. For a woman with as innocent a demeanor as Violet had, she sure knew how to dress to please her man. Nick's face registered delight as he slid his hands up and down the silky fabric covering Violet's legs.

Lifting her onto the edge of the desk, he spread her thighs and moved between them. The look on Violet's face was pure love as Nick drove his cock deep within her. The pair moaned loudly, fortunately drowning out the matching moans of Echo and Alex as their fingers sped up to match the now furious pumping of Nick into Violet.

Under his hand Alex's cock spasmed and his release grew imminent. He slowed, holding off. He didn't want to finish this way, coming in his hand while watching the woman he desired masturbate. Shaking, he carefully replaced his still aching cock into his pants and zipped them up.

Echo leaned against the wall, her fingers delving deeper into her pussy, seeking elusive sexual relief. Violet and Nick moved in well-practiced unison, knowing just what tricks to pull to give each other the ultimate pleasure. Violet nibbled Nick's neck, while he lifted her ass off the table, driving deeper into her. She shuddered and let loose a sharp cry into his neck. He clutched at her, once, twice, then a deep groan erupted from him as he emptied himself into his wife.

At the doorway, Echo cried out as well, a pitiful sound after the joyful noise that Violet had made. She might have found some relief, but Alex knew it hadn't been sufficient. Her face registered frustration as she wiped her fingers on her gown.

Still joined, Violet and Nick leaned together, talking in quiet whispers, their faces radiating love for each other. For a moment Alex watched, drawn by the sight of their intimacy. That's what sex looked like when love was involved. Even in the good days with Mel he'd never had that.

Alex shook his head and stared in the other direction. He wasn't looking for love, didn't want a lover, certainly didn't want to be part of a couple like Violet and Nick. The last time he'd gotten serious about a woman...well, thinking about it wouldn't do any good. Some wounds took a long time to heal, and he wasn't ready to deal with the ones Mel had left behind.

All he wanted was a woman to ease his aching balls, to satisfy his need for a good fuck. Echo was just the woman he wanted—beautiful, with great legs and tits, and she needed satisfaction as much as he did. She couldn't leave the museum and follow him home, wouldn't expect more than what she got from him. When they finished they would part company, no muss, no fuss.

Echo also watched the happy couple cuddling and whispering sweet words to each other. Straightening, she leaned against the doorframe and waved her hand. The door reappeared, solid as it had been. For a moment she stood still, her look defeated, then slowly she moved down the hallway back towards her statue.

Her attitude radiated sadness, and Alex felt a momentary pang of sympathy. She looked like she'd loved and lost someone just as he had. Maybe what he had in mind wasn't such a good idea...he could wind up hurting her, and that wasn't right.

Then again...Echo needed to get laid as much as he did and he wanted her too much to give up. He'd try to convince her to have sex with him. If she refused, so be it, he'd let her go. But if she didn't refuse...it was too tempting to not try.

Keeping out of sight, he followed her.

As she reached the narrow hallway leading to the gallery that held her statue, Echo walked faster and Alex had to run through an adjacent room to get in front of her. He had to be between her and her statue, but they needed to be beyond earshot of Violet and Nick for his plan to work. He arrived at the end of the hall just as she appeared at its other end. He held his breath as she came towards him.

When she reached the middle of the hall, he deliberately cleared his throat. Immediately Echo froze in place and pressed against the wall, her eyes frantic as her gaze searched the darkened hall.

Alex moved out of the shadows and into the hall, moving to within a few feet of her startled form. He tried a reassuring smile that got no response from her other than a further widening of her green eyes.

Well, it was now or never. "Hello, Echo. Having fun?"

Chapter Two

Merciful Aphrodite, the man was *speaking* to her. Worse, he was doing so while she was in solid form. Horrified, Echo stared at the human male in the ugly brown uniform who blocked the hallway in front of her.

No one was ever supposed to see her like this. It was a violation of all the rules and if the gods found out she was using magic to take solid form — not to mention making solid walls disappear — there'd be all sorts of trouble...trouble that she didn't need. Even Aphrodite who'd given her those meager powers wouldn't be able to help her if Hera heard that Echo was on the loose.

She shouldn't have slipped out of her statue, but several weeks ago she'd heard Narcissus's voice for the first time in centuries and hadn't been able to help herself. She'd had to see him. Not even Hera could have kept her from doing so. When it turned out that he was a regular visitor to the museum, she'd been delighted. At first.

But then she'd realized that his visits were to another woman, a woman he loved. By listening carefully, she'd learned that Narcissus had been a statue in the nearby park, and had temporarily become human so he could love a human woman named Violet. Ultimately he'd earned his permanent humanity by convincing the Goddess Aphrodite that he'd learned self-sacrifice. Now renamed Nicolas Rockman, he and Violet were married and even had a child. It was to avoid making too much noise around their little girl that they'd taken to making love late at night in the museum. It was a circumstance much to Echo's prurient delight.

Oh yes, her delight. After three thousand years of not being able to participate herself, she'd been reduced to watching others make love.

It hadn't been that way when she was alive. She'd been a saucy nymph, up for the latest mischief, involved in every gossip. She'd enjoyed life then and to the fullest. Echo had been well-known for her love of the joys of the flesh.

But then Hera had caught her using her chatter to distract the goddess so that Zeus could hide the fact that he was dallying with the other nymphs. She'd lost her voice as a result. That had been bad enough, but later she'd lost her heart. She'd seen Narcissus and fallen in love. Of course he hadn't noticed her. He'd never noticed her all those years ago.

Oh, but she'd noticed him. Even after she lost the ability to speak more than the last few words of any sentence spoken to her, she'd tried to communicate with him. Unfortunately it hadn't worked out as she'd planned.

She remembered it so clearly.

He'd stood by that still pool, staring into the water, entranced by his own reflection, the result of a wicked curse. He'd said, "I love you," into the water.

From behind a tree, she'd repeated the words. It was the only time she'd be able to tell him how she felt.

But he hadn't noticed it was her voice he'd heard. Narcissus had thought his reflected image had told him of its love, and so he fallen deeper into the spell. She'd watched him starve himself by that pond and die his mortal death. When he died she tried to follow him.

But death didn't come easily to a nymph and instead she'd become a shadow of herself, her body fading away leaving nothing but a spirit that wandered the lonely spaces in the world, her voice the only thing left of her.

The Goddess Aphrodite had found a skilled sculptor and convinced him to make a statue in her image, tying Echo's spirit to the mortal world again and giving her a home. She was even allowed the solidity to walk the earth at times, but only if no one knew about it.

Now someone knew, and that someone had spoken to her, words she could repeat back. What had they been again? Oh, yes. *"Hello Echo. Having fun?"*

She stared at him. "Fun?"

His smile grew bigger and he stepped closer. Echo had to crane her neck to look into his face. Great goddess, but he was a big man, even bigger than Narcissus, who hadn't been considered small in his day. Whoever this human was, he had to be over six feet tall.

"Yeah, you know, fun."

"Fun," she said dubiously.

"Sure," the big man said confidently. "Fun, as in watching other people get off."

"Get off?" What did he mean by that? As always, Echo felt a surge of frustration. Once she'd been a great conversationalist and now she was reduced to repeating people's words. It was terrible not being able to say what you want.

"Get off. Like the Rockmans were doing. You know, having sex."

"Having sex?" she repeated in disbelief, her jaw dropping open. "Having *sex!*"

The only way he'd know that she'd watched Narcissus and Violet was if he'd seen her watch them...and if he'd seen that, he'd seen...

Horror filled her. This stranger had seen her with her fingers in her woman's secret place, trying to pleasure herself. She thought nothing could be worse than being caught solid, but this was far more humiliating. Face aflame, she backed away from him.

Immediately his hand went out to rest on the wall next to her keeping her from moving further. "Hey, it's okay. I'm cool. My name is Alex Milton."

"Alex Milton," Echo repeated carefully.

"That's right. Alex. I'm a photography student at the local college. A graduate student."

She had no idea what a photography student did, but it didn't sound threatening. She knew the college was where Narcissus worked and it was a place of higher education. How bad could a student be?

He moved in closer, and she could actually smell him, a man scent mixed with lime and cinnamon. Not a bad smell, just unusual. It made her feel warm and she found herself leaning forward to catch a little more of his aroma.

Alex caught her hand in his and raised it to his face. So awkward...it had been centuries since a man had touched her and she didn't know what to do. His grip was firm, his fingers rough against her skin.

"There's nothing to be afraid of. I'm not going to hurt you, nothing like that. You seemed like you could use some attention, that's all, and you got mine." He kissed her fingers, sliding them across his lips and licking them. She realized they were the ones she'd used in her secret place. He was tasting her musk off her fingertips and he didn't seem to mind at all.

He wrapped his tongue around one of the digits, and for a moment she wondered how it would feel to have him doing that in a more intimate spot.

When she'd watched Nick and Violet, she'd felt a deep stirring inside, a need for...something. Touching herself had relieved some of the tension, but not enough of it. Alex's sucking on her finger brought it all back again, and then some. She moaned as he pulled her finger out of his mouth.

"Oh, babe, you looked so hot touching yourself."

"Hot?" She was certainly feeling hot at the moment, both from her inner core and the warmth radiating off the man in front of her. His gaze seared through her. He glanced down at her breasts. She followed his gaze and saw her nipples rise through the fabric of her gown, pointing at him. Alex licked his lips, his eyes riveted at those slender points.

"Oh, yeah, hot. Let me show you what I mean."

He leaned forward to capture her mouth, kissing her. Lips soft and demanding covered hers, taking her breath away. Echo leaned heavily against the wall, her knees weak after he pulled away from her.

"Listen, I think you have a need for satisfaction, and so do I."

"Satisfaction?"

"Yeah, satisfaction. You know, sex. I want you, I want to have sex with you; I want to make you scream the way she did."

This she understood. He wanted to make her feel like Violet had felt. Echo nodded. "Scream."

"Yeah, babe, scream your lungs out. Why don't we find a place a little more private and I'll give you what you need?"

Her secret spot throbbed into awareness and Echo couldn't resist its wishes any longer. "Need...you," she whispered.

Alex's grin split his face. "Oh, babe, my pleasure. Come with me."

His strong arm around her waist felt wonderful as he directed her to a small room off the main floor. Metal cabinets lined the walls, and along one side was a couch with a large black box on a stand nearby. This is where he led her to sit before leaving to bolt the door.

Alex noticed her looking around the room. "This is the security hangout. There's a TV for the quiet times. I guess the couch is the most comfortable place for doing what we have in mind." He stared at her, almost worshipful. "I can hardly believe you're here."

Echo nodded. She was having a little trouble believing it herself. One minute she'd been on her way back to her statue, and now she was with a man who'd promised to satisfy her. She probably should have refused him, but after watching Narcissus and his lady she wanted to feel what they felt.

Aphrodite might get upset that she'd become solid in front of others, and but as long as the goddess didn't find out...what was the harm?

Alex was still on the other side of the room. If he was going to have sex with her he couldn't do it from there. In his last sentence he'd said, "*I can't believe you're here.*" Oh good, a word she could use. She patted the couch next to her. "Here."

He grinned and took the seat she'd suggested. "You are so beautiful. I wish I had my camera. I'd sure like to take your picture."

Echo let her hand slide against his cheek, sampling the rough texture of his face. "Picture?"

"Yeah, picture. I told you I'm a photography student. Doing the security thing here at the museum is just to make some money while I'm in school. When I get out, I want to shoot pictures professionally. I just need to get together a portfolio, something that will grab the editor's eye."

Smiling, she drew a circle around his eye with her finger. "Grab eye."

"Right, babe. I'm told I've got a great eye, can see stuff through a viewfinder that no one else can, capture it and get it on film. I'm good."

Her finger slid down his nose and came to rest next to his mouth. "Good," she murmured, then leaned over to touch his lips with hers.

He breathed out heavily. "Oh, babe." That was the last intelligible thing he said for a while, but Echo soon realized words weren't necessary. Low moans and soft groans got the message across.

Alex's lips weren't soft. They were full, and strong, and after his surprise wore off at her kissing him first, they became demanding. His strong arms pulled her into his chest, and he pressed her into the back of the couch. His mouth took possession of hers, at one moment devouring, the next teasing. His tongue swept the inside of her mouth and engaged hers in a sensual battle that left her gasping for breath.

This big man was an expert kisser, and she'd kissed some experts in her time. It had been close to three thousand years, but she remembered some pleasant idle moments spent with various mythical figures. She'd even traded kisses with Eros once, long before he'd found his Psyche, the woman who personified his soul.

Now Eros had been an expert kisser!

Not that she'd ever confess that to Aphrodite. The goddess had trouble enough with her son having a wife, much less previous lovers. Sometimes a mother didn't want to see her adult children as capable of adult behaviors.

Maybe Alex wasn't quite the kisser that Eros was, but he wasn't bad at all. What other sensual skills did this big man have? Echo pressed closer to him and felt the hard shaft of his erection through his ugly brown pants. That was definitely promising.

He responded by taking hold of her shoulder, fumbling with the fastenings that held her gown up. In an instant the clasps parted and the top fell, baring her to the waist. Her already raised nipples grew harder as the cool air hit them, bringing them to almost painful points.

His face showing a near-worshipful expression, Alex dipped his head to gently suckle first one and then the other of her breasts. Electricity seemed to flow into her belly, then downward into her secret place. Echo leaned back lifting her breasts higher, giving him better access. She gave herself up to his touch, his worshiping mouth, and let the experience chase away her three thousand years without physical senses.

He was really good at this. Suppose he used that mouth of his elsewhere…

But she was getting ahead of things. If she wanted his mouth on her, she would need to put hers on him. She started unbuttoning his shirt the way she'd watched Narcissus's woman do. It was harder than it looked...she wasn't familiar with the fastenings in this day and age. Slowly she managed to open one, then another.

With an impatient grunt, Alex took over from her, speeding through the rest of his buttons and throwing his shirt on the floor. Grabbing her hands, he placed them on his chest, over the flat brown nipples. Fine golden hair that matched the blond of his scalp glistened in the dim light of the room. Echo fondled his nipples then leaned in to lick them, earning Alex's guttural approval.

If only he'd speak, say something. She wanted to tell him what she felt, but could say nothing without the words he needed to speak first. Frustration filled her at the silence she was bound to.

He lifted her and removed the rest of her gown, then laid her back on the couch. Pushing her legs apart, he stared at her secret place. For an instant she was embarrassed to be so exposed, but then she read the frank admiration and desire in his eyes. He licked his lips, and she remembered how he'd licked her fingers and tasted the womanly juices lingering there. Anticipation rose as he slowly lowered himself to the juncture of her legs.

The first touch of his tongue on that tiny sensitive spot between her legs nearly sent her off the couch, but then he grabbed her hips and held her in place. The second time he licked her forced a sharp cry out of her lips, the third touch set her limbs trembling and left her toes a tingle.

Then Alex got serious, and nibbled, licked, and sucked at her as she writhed beneath him. Sometimes he pulled back to blow on her, cool air that sharpened the sensitized nerves. He slid a finger into her sheath, then added a second, testing her readiness.

She could have told him she was ready. If he'd thought she was hot before, now she felt like she was fire. Heat blazed outward from where his mouth touched her, traveling through her legs to her feet, and her toes that clutched the couch. She raked her fingertips against his bare back, wanting to communicate her fire to him, make him as hot as she felt.

She *needed* him.

He pulled back from her and reached for the fastening of his pants, undoing the metal on his belt. She heard a snicking sound of metal sliding against metal, and then his pants joined her gown and his shirt on the floor. Echo gazed raptly at the long thick length of his man's part, now beckoning to her as if begging for attention.

Slowly she leaned forward to take him into her mouth, first licking the purpled head. It was different from the ones she'd known before, simpler in shape—there was less flesh on it, she realized. It looked…nice.

It tasted nice too. A little salty, like his mouth, a little earthy like his nipples had been. A little bit like his smell, lime and cinnamon. A man's taste and she reveled in it having been denied its flavor for so long.

Some time ago Aphrodite had pointed out to her that three thousand years of mourning Narcissus was quite enough and that Echo might think about continuing her life. Echo wondered now if the goddess might not have a point. Not that she intended to do anything but go back to her statue when they were done here.

But this was very nice, sucking on this strange man's flesh. His appreciative groans gave her a feeling of power.

Each stroke of her tongue made him harder, thicker. Soft whispers came from him, encouragement she thought, but she barely understood their meaning.

Well, she might not understand the words, but the hand on the back of her head, pushing his shaft further into her mouth she understood well enough. She took him deeper, and he groaned, shifted his hips to stroke past her lips, filling her mouth with his hardness and salt-earth taste.

He stopped suddenly and put his hands on her shoulders, stilling her movements, and when she would have taken more of him, he pulled out of her mouth, shaking his head.

"I want you, babe, and I'm ready, but I want to come inside you. That okay with you?"

"That okay," she replied haltingly.

He pushed her shoulders to lay her down, then placed himself between her thighs, the broad tip of his shaft just at her entrance. He pushed forward, stretching her…it had been so long, and he was so large. She tightened against him. He pushed harder, and there was pain. She cried out.

Alex glanced down at her in shock. "You're not a virgin are you?" She shook her head and was surprised to see the relief in his face. Didn't men value virginity here?

"Thank goodness. I didn't think I'd be the first, but you're a lot tighter than I expected."

He pulled out of her and returned to suckling her nipples, using his dampened fingers to ease her opening wider, giving her more pleasure than she'd experienced even when she'd been a carefree nymph. Gradually the muscles of her sheath relaxed, while other tensions rose.

With an impatient hand she grabbed his fingers, pulling them from her body. She took them into her mouth, tasting herself, and spread her legs wider beneath him.

Alex grinned at her, a sensual grin of knowing amusement. "You think you're ready for me, huh?"

His fingers, talented as they were, just were not big enough. She needed something much bigger, longer, and fatter. "Ready," she told him. "Ready."

Again Alex placed himself and pushed, and this time did it harder. When she tightened, he fingered her sensitive place. The sensation drove her into climax and when she returned to herself he was embedded deep within her.

He was breathing heavily. "Babe, you've got the tightest pussy I've ever felt."

"Pussy?" Not a word she knew.

"Yeah, pussy, slit, cunt, although that's not a nice enough word for yours. Yours is a pussy, sweet, hot, and tight. Feels good." He moved a little.

Echo gasped at the sensation. Hot and sweet, indeed. "Feels good," she moaned.

Alex braced himself on his arms, staring down at her. "Hang on, babe. It's going to get serious now." He pulled back and pushed forward, sliding deeper inside her, then repeated the stroke. His hips set up a rhythm Echo found herself matching, push for pull, stoke for stroke. Their movement caught fire, and the small climaxes she'd experienced before repeated themselves, but in succession, each building on top of the other.

Inside her she felt a strangeness, as if a thread stretched tight, nearly to a breaking point. Echo caught her breath, and gazed up at Alex, his eyes glazed and face intense. A low growl came from him, guttural and almost animalistic, and then he gave a harsh cry. He sped up.

The thread inside her snapped as Echo slipped off into her own climax, her scream muffled by Alex's chest.

Above her head he roared into the cushions and within her she felt his shaft pulsing, sending his seed deep into her womb.

Chapter Three

For a while neither of them could speak. Alex had collapsed on top of her, and now lay very still, breathing heavily in her ear.

A warm, happy glow filled Echo. She stroked the man's cheek lying next to hers. Never before had she felt this kind of peace when having sex. What could be the reason? Still shaking from the intensity of her orgasm, she labored for air, each breath harsh in her throat. The air felt different somehow, heavier. When she was solid it always seemed odd to breathe but this was worse than usual. Now she could barely catch her breath.

Some of her warm glow faded, leaving her feeling strange. Very strange, that was for certain, strange and oddly out of sorts.

"Wow, babe...that was fantastic."

"Fantastic," she repeated. Well, it had been the most intense sex she'd had in three thousand years, but the terrific feeling she had was fading fast. Something was definitely wrong.

Alex laughed. "Yeah, fantastic. I can't believe it was so easy."

Her uneasiness found a focus. She did not like how Alex was laughing. It almost sounded as if he was laughing at her. "Easy?"

He didn't seem to notice her irritation. "Too easy, babe. I expected to have to convince you and you just came right along."

"Convince?" He'd thought she needed convincing and had a plan for it?

Alex raised himself on his arms and stared down at her. As much as she appreciated the admiration in his eyes, the smug smile on his face wasn't improving her mood. "Well, yeah. I mean who'd expect a babe like you would be so eager to get laid. I thought I'd have to talk you into it, maybe even threaten to tell the Rockmans that you were spying on them."

Horror filled her. "Tell the Rockmans?" This man who'd just made love to her had been intending to tell Narcissus that she'd watched him and Violet? He would have used that to get her to do what he wanted?

Alex must have read her expression and figured out she wasn't taking this news well. He put a placating hand on her shoulder. "Hey take it easy, babe."

Echo pushed on his shoulder, and off-balance as he was, Alex fell off the couch. He sat bare-assed on the floor, staring at her in astonishment. Springing to her feet, Echo grabbed her gown from the pile of clothing and fled for the door. After unbolting it and swinging it open, she turned to glare at him.

"Not easy babe!" she shouted before taking off down the hall, heading for her statue.

She was halfway there before she realized she'd used the word "not" in her last sentence —

—*and he hadn't!*

* * * * *

Oh, crap. Damn, shit, crap. Alex scrambled into his clothes, trying to button his shirt with one hand while pulling on his underwear and pants with the other. How could he have been so stupid? Here he'd had the best sexual experience in months…

Okay, scratch that, even with Mel-the-Bitch it hadn't been that great. Here he'd had the best sex in years…

No, even that wasn't enough. He couldn't remember ever having sex that good at all. Fucking Echo had been the best fucking ever. It had been world-championship fucking, on a level he'd never seen before.

If the Olympics had a competition for sex, he and Echo would have just won the gold medal for pairs.

He'd never felt so close to a woman, any woman, like he'd been with her.

And he'd just told his number-one sex partner of all time that she'd been too easy.

Damn, shit, fuck, CRAP!

Alex gave up on buttoning the shirt and left it open, pulling on his shoes instead. He had to reach her statue before she got inside and was lost to him forever. He had to at least apologize, or she'd never speak to him again.

Not that she spoke much now, only repeating the last words he said. That was kind of cool when you thought about it, having a girlfriend who couldn't say more than you did. If you never said, "I love you", she'd never say it either.

Alex shook his head. He wasn't looking for a girlfriend, was he? No, not at all. But he couldn't just leave it as it was with Echo. He'd never forgive himself. She hadn't deserved to be hurt that way.

Leaving the security office, he slammed the door and ran down the hall.

* * * * *

Echo reached the gallery. Ahead was her statue, gleaming in the dim after-hours lighting. Echo rushed to it, then spent a few moments slipping on her gown and fastening the golden clasps. Butterflies, they were beautiful in design, a gift from her sister, Nemesis. She secured the hooks, then straightened her gown so it matched the statue in front of her.

The feeling of not-rightness continued, and it made her nervous. She fussed with the gown more than she usually did before merging back into her stone home.

She realized that she was delaying the inevitable and wondered why. What was she doing, waiting for the oaf she'd had sex with to catch up with her and apologize? He'd laughed at her, called her names, said she was "easy" to talk into sex. She might not have spent much time as a solid in the past three thousand years, but she knew an insult when she heard it. He didn't respect her, not at all.

Not that she respected herself very much. Even the memory of that wonderful warm glow she'd had after they'd finished failed to cheer her. She had been too easy for him to talk into sex.

No matter, it was over. She would just step forward and merge into her statue. Still nervous, Echo reached out her arms, closed her eyes, and stepped forward to meld with the stone in front of her.

WHAP!

Moaning, Echo rubbed her aching nose. It had collided with the solid marble. This was the second painful thing to happen to her today, and she never felt pain. She never felt anything usually.

First had been when Alex had tried to enter her and she wasn't ready, and then when he'd called her easy...

No, that was the second time. Hitting the marble was the third time. Three painful incidents in one night...she should never have become solid tonight, not even to watch Narcissus making love to Violet. The whole evening had gone wrong, and it was all Alex's fault.

The feeling of not-rightness got stronger. Never had she'd bumped her nose when re-entering the statue. All she had to do was think transparent, the same as she did with the door to Violet's office.

Just think transparent, give up her solidity and become a spirit again. Echo opened her arms and thought light thoughts. She was mist, an indistinct shadow, nothing more than thought...she would enter her marble representation and lose herself in the spirit world...

...she stepped forward.

WHAP!

Crying in pain, Echo knelt on the floor, one hand nursing her injured nose. Something dripped onto her hand. She checked and saw blood on her fingers. *A bloody nose?* She had a bloody nose from trying to go back into her statue!

Echo leaned against the stone figure and gave herself up to despair. What was she going to do? She was trapped here in a world with lovers who called you easy when they got what they wanted.

She was crying so hard, she missed the swirl of random dust moving off the floor, turning into a whirlwind. The whirlwind rose in the middle of the room and departed as quickly as it came, leaving behind a beautiful figure of a woman, with long blonde hair and the most exquisite cheekbones.

Aphrodite, fairest of the fair, goddess of carnal love, beauty, and desire had made her entrance. Smiling, she regarded the miserable nymph in front of her, completely overcome with grief and loss.

She held aloft the crystal wineglass in her hand and tapped it with a long polished fingernail. The bell-like sound caught Echo's attention and instantly she jumped to her feet. She bowed with as much dignity as she could, hampered by keeping one hand on her nose, trying to staunch the bleeding.

Out of thin air, the goddess plucked a silk handkerchief and handed it to the unfortunate nymph. "Goodness, you're a mess. Put pressure on it, dear, and tilt your head forward." She nodded approvingly as Echo followed her instructions. "There now, that should fix it."

Glancing around, Aphrodite noticed the marble bench at the edge of the room. Gracefully she glided to it and settled her slender frame on one end. The wine in her glass barely sloshed as she sat down.

After straightening her gown, she turned her attention to Echo, head still tilted down, watching her with bated breath. She smiled and patted the bench next to her.

"Now, dear, I believe there is something we should talk about."

Echo lowered her head and checked the handkerchief. Thank goodness, the bleeding seemed to have stopped.

Screwing up her courage, she sat on the bench as directed. "Talk about?"

The goddess finished her wine and tossed the goblet into the air, where it promptly disappeared. "Yes, talk about. It seems there are congratulations in order." Smiling broadly, she applauded with both hands.

Confused, Echo stared at the goddess. "Congratulations?"

"Of course, congratulations. You've lifted your curse."

"Curse? How?"

Abruptly she realized that "how" hadn't been one of the words Aphrodite had used. "How?" she said again, softly.

"By having sex with a mortal and making him love you; that's how you've won your freedom. The curse you were under is lifted; you're human now and can talk, although the last may take some time to get used to. With practice I'm sure you'll be just fine."

Astonished, Echo's mouth dropped open. She could talk again? The implications whirled through her mind. She'd be able to form sentences without using someone else's words. First sentences! She could start a conversation and not have to wait until someone else spoke first.

Why, she'd be able to tell that jerk Alex exactly what she thought of him, and use words she was certain he'd never think of using first. Her face grew warm at the image of that triumph.

Not that she'd really do it. After all, she was going back into her statue and she'd never speak to him again…

Wait a minute. What was that other part of what Aphrodite said? Echo turned to the goddess. To her dismay, the words she needed for her question were still hard to find.

"Human?" she finally got out.

The goddess beamed. "Yes, you're human now. Isn't that wonderful?"

Wonderful? No, it wasn't wonderful. She was a nymph, a mythical demi-creature, immune to the travails of humankind. If she were human she'd be mortal, she could get sick…

Horror struck her. She could get *pregnant*!

"Aphrodite," she struggled out. "Me…human."

Benevolently the goddess patted her on the shoulder. "I know it's all a bit overwhelming but you needn't thank me right now. It was my idea, you know, to put that test before you. I knew that once you tasted actual passion, you'd be thrilled and never want to go back."

Oh she was thrilled all right, if by thrilled the goddess meant terrified right down to her tiptoes. But what was she going to do? She pointed to the statue, her home for so many centuries. "Go back," she asked, putting all her want into her voice.

A perplexed expression came over Aphrodite's face. "You mean you *do* want to return to the statue? Aren't you pleased to be human after all this time?"

In answer Echo burst into tears. The goddess moved closer and wrapped her arms around the unfortunate girl. Patting her gently on the back, she shook her head in consternation. "Dear, dear…I didn't expect you to take it this way. Why Narcissus was thrilled, but then he'd had his love there with him."

"Not love," she managed to get out between sobs. "Not love me."

"Oh, dear." The goddess didn't like that at all. A frown developed on her perfect lips. "Well, that's got to change. This spell only works if there is everlasting love involved. Otherwise you'll only stay human for a few weeks, two months at best and then return to being what you were."

Back to what she was? But she wanted that, didn't she?

Aphrodite continued on as if she'd heard her thoughts and Echo decided that most likely she could. "You might not be able to go back to being a statue though. You could even go back to the oblivion you were in before the statue was made. It would depend on whether or not you were near the statue when the spell fails."

She patted Echo's hand. "The last time you lost form was because you failed to win Narcissus's love and it wasted you away. But that was thousands of years ago and surely you've learned how to make a man love you now. After all, at least this time you got him to make love with you. That's a good first step."

She might go back to oblivion? No, Echo *really* didn't want to go back there. She'd do anything to avoid that. Even learn how to make Alex love her. Echo felt the cold marble under her. It was nice to be able to feel again...even if the marble was cold enough to remind her of the half-life she'd experienced before.

"So you see, the situation is this. You have to make Alex fall in love with you. If you can, you'll live happily as a human. Otherwise you'll fade back into oblivion and have to go back to the statue."

Aphrodite arched a perfect eyebrow. "Of course you can't tell him that, he has to fall in love on his own without any threats."

She raised Echo's chin with the edge of her graceful hand, staring into the former nymph's face, a hint of menace in her own. "So, where is that young man of yours?"

At the sound of running footsteps in the hall, both women turned to the gallery doorway. Still struggling to fasten his belt, his shirttail not completely tucked in, and one foot wearing a shoe but no sock, Alex appeared in the entrance. His face was flushed and he breathed heavily, out of breath. He startled at the sight of the pair sitting on the bench and Echo thought she saw a trace of guilty dismay cross his handsome features.

Wiping her tears away, she glared at him. *Good, he should feel guilty.* Thanks to him, she was no longer able to hide away from the world and would have to learn how to live as a human. What's worse, she'd have to make him love her. They'd have to spend lots of time having sex...

His eyes lit up when he saw her sitting there and it made her feel warm and tingly, just as she had when she'd first realized his attraction for her. Maybe having a lot of sex wouldn't be all that bad.

"You must be Echo's young man. So *happy* to meet you."

Angry as she was with Alex, Echo cringed at the goddess's tone. Aphrodite didn't sound the least bit happy, and an unhappy goddess was a dangerous thing. There were stories about how Violet's abusive ex-boyfriend had ended up replacing Narcissus—that is, Nick—as a statue in the park.

Alex crossed his arms and scowled, and Echo had to resist the urge to cry out to him to be careful. Not that she really cared what happened to him, the miserable pig. It was just that she didn't need him to end up as stone, or some sort of animal like an ass — or a pig. She had to make him love her and a man of stone or a pig just wouldn't do that.

"Who are you? And what are you doing in the museum? We're closed."

A beautiful smile crossed Aphrodite's face, a smile that went nowhere near her eyes. "Very few places are closed to one such as myself. I have my ways in and out. As for what I'm doing here, I'm visiting Echo, a dear little friend of mine. A *very* dear friend. I was just giving her the good news."

"Good news?" Alex looked confused.

"Yes. She's free, of the statue and the curse. She can live like a normal person now."

"She can?" Alex's gaze landed on Echo. Was that interest in his eyes? "She doesn't need to go back into the statue?"

"Can't go back," Echo replied haltingly. She still couldn't find the words she wanted, and the struggle irritated her.

"I know how that is. Sometimes you can't go back home, no matter what."

Echo looked up in surprise. She heard sympathy in his voice. He looked at her in concern and the warm feeling she'd had when they'd finished making love returned.

Maybe making him fall in love with her wouldn't be that bad at all.

The goddess tapped her golden sandal on the marble floor. "Indeed, she must leave the museum. This is no place for a living woman to dwell. And, since she must leave, she must have a destination. She'll need a place to sleep and live. She'll need someone to help her adjust to this new world."

A thoughtful look came over her face. "There is Nick, of course. And Violet. I suppose they could help her."

Nick? Violently Echo shook her head. There was no way she could live with her former love and his lover. It would be so humiliating.

"No?" The goddess acknowledged Echo's distress. "I guess that would be awkward. But no one told you to spy on them, dear."

Echo groaned. Alex had seen her, and now she knew Aphrodite was aware of her transgression as well. Did everyone know about her little indiscretion?

The beautiful goddess patted her hand. "Not everyone, dear. But you should be more careful when using magic. It does tend to attract a crowd. But this isn't settling where you're going to live. You can't stay here, and you can't go out on your own. Staying with Nick and his wife doesn't suit you. So where are you to go? Who's going to help you learn to be a woman in this world?"

She turned to stare meaningfully at Alex. His eyes widened and face paled as the implications of her question sunk in. Wildly his gaze darted between Echo and the goddess, panic rising in his face. It was the look of a trapped animal.

"Um…well…" he stammered out.

Echo's heart sank. They'd made love just minutes ago, and now he couldn't bear the thought of taking her into his home. It was hopeless trying to make him love her. Now that he'd had sex with her, he didn't want her again.

"Go get Nick." Echo managed to get out, and turned her attention to her bare feet, cold against the marble floor. For the first time she noticed how cool it was in the gallery and how thin her gown was. She shivered and rubbed her arms.

"You want me to get Nick, my dear?" the goddess asked solicitously, putting a comforting arm around her shoulders. "I'm sure he and Violet would help you."

"No…" Alex said the word slowly, as if it were being dragged out of him. "She can go with me."

Perfectly curved twin eyebrows rose in unison on the goddess's face. "Are you sure, Alexander? We wouldn't want to put you to any trouble."

If he recognized the dangerous sarcasm in Aphrodite's voice, he chose to ignore it. Echo decided he just didn't notice it.

"Yeah, it will be all right. I've got room," he said reluctantly. He consulted his watch. "I don't get off work until six, but you could hang out in the security room until then."

Another shiver ran through Echo and she bent to rub her feet. They were freezing!

A shadow fell over her and she looked up to see a mix of concern and worry on Alex's face. He held out his hand to her. "You must be cold. There are a couple of blankets in one of the lockers and I've got a thermos of coffee. Let's go back to the office and get you warmed up."

After staring at his outstretched palm for what felt like forever, Echo tentatively placed her hand on top of his.

Alex pulled her up and led her out of the hall, one arm around her shoulders.

Apparently forgotten by the pair, Aphrodite watched them leave, a sly smile stealing across her face.

"This is going to be fun," she said quietly to herself.

"Fun for whom, Aphrodite?"

The harsh but seductive male voice made her turn, her eyes narrowing as she spotted its source. From the shadows stepped a figure, folding his arms across the coarse hair of his massive chest. A narrow strip of fabric covered his loins, but otherwise he was garbed only in hair, from the top of his head to the thick curly pelt on his legs, which had an odd shape to them, more the legs of a goat than a man. As he moved forward, a soft clip-clop echoed in the hall, the sound of cloven hoofs against a marble floor.

His face was handsome in spite of the narrow unkempt beard, with compelling eyes whose expression matched the frown on his sensuous down-turned lips. Nestled in the short curly brown hair on his head were two horns, tiny and barely visible.

She kept her voice amused as though his presence wasn't an issue. "Pan, god of the woodlands and fields. What are you doing in an urban setting like this?"

"I seek what was stolen from me. Echo the nymph was mine to have, given to me."

"She was given to the forests, Pan, as all nymphs were. You could dally with them, but only if they were willing. She wasn't willing, if I remember it correctly."

"She was *stolen* from me," he repeated angrily. "Stolen by that lout, Narcissus, whose love she couldn't win." He reached to touch the statue of Echo, her image in stone, discarded for the moment. He stroked the arm of the figure with an injured air.

"She let herself fade to nothing as a result, rejecting me who would have given her the attention she craved."

Aphrodite folded her own perfect arms and glared at the god. "You know that love doesn't work that way, Pan. Just because one forces love on another doesn't mean that they will return it. Echo found that out with Narcissus, you should learn it too."

Pan's hand drew back from the statue and became a fist. "I won't give up so easily, nor will I fade to nothing or turn to stone." He returned the goddess's glare. "You think that Echo will find love with this human man, but he will disappoint her just like all men do. When that happens she will seek the same oblivion she had before, but I'll be waiting for her. Let him teach her to appreciate the sensual arts…no one is as good at those as I am."

As if to illustrate his point, Pan pressed himself against the statue and ground his crotch with loving skill along its backside. When he stepped back, Aphrodite could see the long ridge his engorged cock made inside his loincloth. In spite of herself, the goddess was impressed.

"I'll win her, you wait and see."

He disappeared into dust as suddenly as he'd appeared, leaving Aphrodite with a hint of a smile on her face.

This could even be more interesting than she'd thought.

Chapter Four

Alex wrapped the blanket around Echo's shoulders and settled her back on the couch. Pouring a mug full of coffee, he held it out to her. Her hand shook as she reached for it, and he had to hold it for her as she took first one hesitant sip, then another. Surprise and appreciation was in her face as she finally took the mug from him and held it to her chest.

"It's good?" he asked her.

"Good," she repeated, nodding. Alex watched as some of the color returned to her face, although she still seemed pale, a thin wispy figure sitting on the couch.

Was this the same woman who'd been with him just an hour ago, who'd screamed her pleasure as they'd made love? And then, later, she'd shouted at him that she wasn't an "easy babe". There'd been a spirit in her then, a strength of purpose.

She seemed so uncertain now. Of course, she'd expected to return to her statue and now she couldn't and that had to be a difficult change for her. She had to learn to be a human woman.

Echo took several deep sips and appeared to melt into the cushions. The look she gave him made him distinctly uneasy. It was a "you're my hero" kind of look, the kind of look a guy got that was supposed to make him want to do something for a girl.

Ah, heck. He did want to do something for her. And to her. And with her, on the couch, or on a desk...

Suppressing a groan, Alex closed up his thermos and stuck it back into his locker. What was he going to do? He'd agreed to take her back to his place in the morning, and help her learn how to be a modern woman. The first was easy. It might even be kind of fun to have her around...

No! He had to stop thinking about her that way. Sex was how he'd got into this mess in the first place. If he'd let her go back to her statue without making love to her, then she'd be as she had been and he wouldn't have her to worry about.

Of course, then he'd still have an erection hard enough to pound nails. Right now he was actually somewhat...well... satisfied. It had been a long time since he'd been with a woman, and he couldn't remember any time that he'd had this kind of pleasure. Even now he couldn't help the stirring in his groin.

He still wanted her, bundled in a blanket and clutching her cup of coffee. She looked so cold — maybe he could warm her up...

Shaking his head, he tried to dispel the thoughts of laying her down on the couch and making love to her again. It would make her warmer, but keep him from his job. He needed to make his rounds of the museum.

"I'll be back in a little while. You stay here and rest."

Fear filled her eyes, but she nodded bravely. "Stay here and rest." She held up her cup. "Good."

Words were still hard for her to come by, but Alex knew what she meant. "Don't worry, babe. I'll be back." He headed for the door.

Echo watched him go, controlling her anxiety over being left alone. After all, she'd been alone most of her life...such as that had been. In the past three thousand years, she'd rarely spent time with others. Only Nemesis, her sister, had come by to visit and even then the conversation had been one-sided. Between being linked to a block of stone and not being able to form her own sentences, she'd generally just listened to her sister rail about this or that without putting in any input of her own.

That was pretty much the fate of an object of art, to be seen and not heard.

At least that was over with. She, the infamous Echo, could talk now, and did she have a lot to say! Or at least she would, once she remembered the words.

She tried a little more of the coffee Alex had given her. It really was quite hot and her first taste had nearly scalded her tongue. This time she sipped just a little of the beverage from her cup, letting it linger in her mouth until it was cool enough to swallow.

It really did have a rich taste, just like everyone said. Over the years she'd heard so many people talk about coffee, particularly those who worked at the museum on their way back to their offices. They would rave about how it smelled, how it tasted, and how much they would give for a really good cup right now. The way they talked, the way they got so excited, it might have been sex they were talking about.

Echo sniffed the cup in front of her. It did have a nice smell. She took another sip and resisted the urge to moan her appreciation. *Well, maybe not quite as good as sex...but close.* And it was hot, the cup warming her hands. As it traveled into the pit of her stomach, empty all these years, it became a centerpiece of heat spreading outward. She'd been so cold, she hadn't realized how much. Now she felt warm, cozy in her blanket.

She finished the last of her coffee and reached to put the cup on the low table next to the couch. Weariness crept along her limbs, dulling her mind. Not quite the dull emptiness of becoming one with her statue, but familiar anyway. Echo yawned, only remembering at the last moment to cover her mouth.

It had been so long since she was alive. She would have to watch herself to avoid embarrassing blunders, actions rude in the modern world. So much to learn.

Would Alex really let her stay with him long enough for her to gain his love? Echo had her doubts. He would have to see it was in his interest to keep her there. She knew he liked sex. At least she could keep his interest that way for a while, but soon that wouldn't be enough. Men tired of women they only used for sex…she'd have to come up with other ways to make him want to keep her until he fell in love with her.

At least for now she was safe. Drawing the blanket around her, Echo rested her head against the small hard pillow behind her, and for the first time in centuries let sleep claim her.

She was still asleep when Alex returned near dawn to take her home.

Alex's car was a beat-up sedan that had clearly seen better days. The color was a faded metallic green and the cracked black vinyl inside smelled old and dusty. Still wearing a blanket as a cloak, Echo climbed into the passenger side. She startled when he reached over her and fastened the seatbelt around her. Never before had she been secured into a seat, and for a moment she wondered why he felt the precaution was necessary.

He took off out of the parking lot of the museum and swung the car into the early morning traffic, and she quit wondering. The ride to Alex's "place" was unnerving, scary, and thrilling all at once. Echo dug her fingernails into the armrest as they sped down the highway at what seemed like a breakneck speed. Never before had she moved so fast! When her statue had been transported, she'd been locked away inside of it and unaware of the world speeding around her.

She felt Alex's gaze when they stopped at an intersection. A frown crossed his face. "Are you okay? You look kind of pale." His eyes widened. "You aren't going to be sick, are you?"

The coffee she'd drunk hours ago rose from the pit of her stomach and she grabbed the armrest tighter, fighting the sensation.

"Okay... not sick," she told him, and prayed it would be true. The last thing she needed was to be ill in Alex's car. She pointed outside, mimicking with her fingers the world moving past her window. "So fast..."

His frown deepened, but when they moved on, he drove slower, and took the curves more cautiously. Echo breathed a sigh of relief when they finally pulled in front of a long two-story building and came to a stop.

She peered up at the vast, uninspiring brick front broken by small windows. One door opened into the place. "Your home? It's so large!"

A short laugh escaped him. "Sorry to disappoint you, but I don't own the whole building. All I have is a small one-bedroom apartment on the second floor, nothing fancy."

Clutching the blanket around her, Echo followed him into the building and up the stairs to stop outside the door as he fumbled with his keys. As little time as she'd known him, she thought Alex looked anxious. Finally he got the door open and let her step inside.

"It's so…" Echo faltered, trying to find in her limited vocabulary the words to describe the sight before her. "…full," she finally said.

Grimacing, Alex threw his keys on the table just inside the door. "Yeah, well…it's kind of been the maid's day off for the past several months."

What did that mean? She moved past piles of papers and dirty clothes that littered the floor. A couch held more clothes, and books and papers. Large flat cardboard boxes smelling of leftover spices had been left on the low table in front of it. To one side a narrow counter separated what seemed to be a food preparation area, with a sink and oven. Storage areas covered the wall above, all of which must be empty since everything that should have been put away was either piled on the countertop or occupied the sink.

Alex led her into a smaller room he called a bathroom. It held white porcelain fixtures, one of which he explained was used for physical relief. At least that was the gist of his explanation, once she understood what piss and crap meant. To her surprise she actually needed to use it, probably the result of the coffee she'd drunk earlier.

Alex was waiting for her after she emerged from the bathroom. Behind him was a large black plastic bag, and much of the trash that had littered the place was gone. The couch was empty, its contents having been moved to the floor nearby, a sheet and blanket decorating it.

Disappointed, Echo stared at the makeshift bed. She'd looked into the room at the end of the hall and seen the large bed that Alex obviously used. Apparently she wasn't going to share it with him.

"Mine?" she pointed at the couch.

He shook his head. "No, I'm giving you the bed in my room."

"No need. Share."

"No share." He stopped. "Look, what happened between us was a mistake. I'm not looking for a girlfriend right now. My life is complicated enough as it is."

"Mistake?"

She couldn't keep the hurt from her voice and he grimaced at it. "Look, I'm sorry. I'll put you up, but I don't want us to get serious. What happened was supposed to be just for fun."

"For fun." She tried a reassuring smile. "I know fun."

"Yeah, I guess you do. All those old Greeks spent a lot of time just having sex for fun from the sound of things."

Yeah, just for fun. But it didn't always stay that way. Some god got really possessive, especially when they didn't get their way. Take Pan for example...

But no, thinking about Pan wasn't going to improve this situation at all. Thank heavens he'd finally given up trying to possess her.

"Fun good. Sleep together good."

"This isn't up for debate...you're sleeping in my room and I'm on the couch." He rubbed his face, weariness obvious in his stance. "I'm too tired to argue more."

Directing her into the bedroom with a firm push of his arm, Alex opened a drawer and pulled out a large white shirt. "Here's a t-shirt for you to sleep in. Be a good girl and go to bed so I can get some rest."

Defiantly Echo dropped her gown to the floor, standing naked in front of him. Alex might have been tired and claiming disinterest, but she saw the quick widening of his eyes and how he caught his breath. A quick glance below his belt gave her further evidence as he turned and stomped out of the room, slamming the door behind him.

Echo smiled to herself. He was still interested.

She pulled the t-shirt over her head. It fell to halfway down her thighs. Good enough for a nightdress, at least for now. Turning back the covers of the wide bed, she slipped between them to luxuriate on the cool sheets. They weren't clean; she could smell Alex's scent on the pillow, thick and musky. Desire rose, hot and intense, and she ached between her legs.

Echo groaned. Just the man's smell was an aphrodisiac. She needed him, no matter how he felt about her, and for more than just the roof over her head or the t-shirt on her back. Staying in his home was going to be a torture if he didn't accept her as a bed partner from the beginning. She'd have to convince him of that — and there was no time like the present to do so!

She heard Alex stumbling around, apparently getting ready for bed. Creeping out the bed, Echo went to the door and opened it crack to listen. There was a soft thud of a knee hitting the low table followed by a mumbled curse, and then the couch creaked as if something heavy stretching out on it. After a while she heard a heavy sigh.

She waited until his breathing grew even before slipping through the door into the living room. The room was in shadows, the heavy drapes across the windows filtering out the early morning light. In the gloom Alex was a dark lump on the couch. Echo crept closer and saw that while his head rested comfortably on a pillow, his legs were too long for the couch. He'd solved the problem by sticking his feet over the end of the sofa where they hung in the air.

Echo pondered the situation. He'd have a crick in his back for certain if he continued to try and sleep that way. Alex was cranky enough as it was…the last thing she needed was him acting like an old bear with a sore back. She should seduce him back to his bed for his own good.

Resolution in her step, Echo moved to the couch and crouched next to him.

Alex had removed his shirt and pants, and lay covered only by a thin blanket. It was bunched up over his crotch…or was that bulge all him and not the blanket?

She let one tentative hand reach to discover the truth. Not only did the bulge get bigger, but Alex made a small moan in his sleep. Alex might be tired, but he was still interested in her. Or at least he was interested in sex, which was good enough for now.

Carefully she peeled back the covers. When they'd made love earlier she'd hadn't had a chance to really look at his body. Now with him asleep, the hard planes of his chest and flat belly were available for her examination, and she took advantage of the opportunity.

He was much older than the usual men she'd seen. Memories of the lithe bodies of the village youths she'd dabbled with and the rock-hard torsos of the various gods who'd been her lovers so long ago faded in the reality of this man. His chest was wide, with a coarse dusting of hair that traveled down to his waist in a narrowing trail. His belly was hard, but had a small softness to it, and there were hints of more softness at the edges of his waist. He looked strong, but well-fed.

Here was a man who worked out, but still enjoyed his dinner. A man with appetites for more than just sex.

Perhaps there would be more than one way to win this man's heart. From the smell of the trash that had littered the place, Alex was living off pre-made food. It had been a long time since Echo had prepared a meal and she'd need to learn how to work the complicated equipment in his kitchen. A challenge but not an insurmountable one.

In the meantime, the bulge still under his blanket jerked again. Alex was dreaming and it wasn't about food.

Echo finished pulling back the covers to find that he'd left his shorts on. She could see his nascent erection, stretching the tight, thin fabric. She blew on the tip and watched the fabric darken with pre-cum.

Again Alex moaned and stretched, one arm falling across his face, covering his eyes. His erection stretched too, nearly filling his undergarment. It looked uncomfortable. Probably it would be a good thing for her to free him from such confinement.

Moving slowly to avoid waking him, Echo slid her hand under the waistband and lifted it. His erect cock sprang out with such force that she nearly let go of the elastic. Thankfully she hadn't or it might have snapped back onto him...that would have woken him up for certain!

Freed, his cock waved proudly in her face, transparent droplets forming on its purple head. Echo stared. It wasn't like Alex's cock was the largest she'd seen—after all, she'd been chased by Pan more than once—but there was something very attractive about it.

Very attractive. She could hardly wait to pet it. Carefully easing his waistband to lie below his privates, Echo gave herself room to work. She ran a careful hand from the tip to the base and back again. Outside of another low moan, Alex didn't seem aware of her explorations.

She played with the fluid leaking from the narrow tip, using that to lubricate her hand. Spreading his own essence along his shaft, she made it possible to fondle him without pulling the skin. Still careful not to overly disturb him, she closed her hand over his cock and stroked it from base to tip.

Alex moaned deeper, but still didn't wake. Encouraged, Echo stepped up her efforts, now using two hands. The purple tip swung before her face and without thinking Echo placed a delicate kiss on it. It tasted lovely.

Seeking more of that deliciousness, she closed her lips over his cock, still using her hand to stroke the base of the shaft. He was far too big to take completely in her mouth. Alex's hips moved in time with her efforts, grinding against her.

She felt so powerful. Never before had she seduced a man, always she'd been the one pursued. There was something blatantly erotic about being the aggressor, about taking what she wanted from a man.

Alex moaned and his hands found her head, caressing her hair. "Oh, yes…like that. Oh, yeah…" His voice was disjointed, still very sleepy, but clearly rousing. Echo stepped up her exertions. She had to make him come before he woke up!

Inside her mouth his cock pulsed, once then twice. He stiffened all over, then cried out while her mouth filled with his come. She swallowed the salt-earth fluid and wiped her mouth with the back of her hand before looking up to see his eyes wide open, staring at her.

"What the fuck was that?" he said when he'd gotten his breath.

She tried to withhold a giggle and failed. "Share bed."

Alex sat up and glared at her. "You went down on me to get me to share a bed with you? Is that it?"

She nodded. He spoke under his breath, words she wasn't familiar with, but she doubted they were compliments.

"Of all the aggravating, irritating, stubborn… There are rules about this sort of thing. How would you like it if I went down on you while you were asleep…?" he broke off as she giggled at him. "I guess you wouldn't much mind that."

He tossed the covers off and stood up, his now complacent cock lying outside his underwear. With an impatient gesture he adjusted his pants to put it away.

"I have class all afternoon today and need to get some sleep, Echo. If I go to bed with you, will you promise to leave me alone?"

At her nod, he grabbed his pillow and headed for the bedroom. "Okay then, we'll share a bed, but I don't want anymore funny business from you. If someone is going to do the seducing around here, it's going to be me. Understand?"

Echo followed him down the hall to the bedroom, trying to conceal her feeling of triumph. If Alex wanted to be the aggressor in their relationship, that was fine with her.

Just as long as they both got laid.

Chapter Five

Television sucked. Wearing one of Alex's t-shirts and a pair of loose-fitting underpants that she'd had to pin in place, Echo used the narrow black box Alex had called a remote, and flipped through the various channels. He'd shown her how to work the TV before leaving for school, but hadn't bothered to explain where anything interesting would be.

She understood the concept. It was like having a series of plays available at the push of a button. Hundreds and hundreds of plays and hours and hours of entertainment. Thousands of people must have been involved in the creation of these shows to provide millions of people with amusement.

And all of it sucked.

After three thousand years of being locked in a statue, she hadn't expected to find life as a mortal boring. She was wrong—she was bored.

Well, not everything was boring. Echo grinned to herself. Waking up with Alex this morning had definitely *not* been boring. After her "going down" on him, he'd given up sleeping on the couch and joined her in his bed. At first he hadn't seemed to want to touch her, but when she'd woken he'd been holding her close, his erection a solid rod nestling between her ass cheeks.

That rod of his had taken very little time in finding a home inside her. Alex growled like a wild beast as he'd taken her from behind. Then he'd pulled her onto her knees and taken her that way, then turned her over and taken her that way...

In the first hour of waking they'd explored at least half of her sexual repertoire. If Alex's alarm clock hadn't gone off, signaling his need to get to class, they'd have probably covered the other half.

Beds in this day and age were wonderful for having sex on. She'd never been as comfortable while on her back before. Or knees for that matter.

But then Alex had left her on her own. She had strict instructions not to leave the apartment or answer the telephone. He'd shown her how to use the television as an afterthought, suggesting that listening to the voices would help improve her language.

He was right. Now she could say "Ask your physician if Zantha will work for you" — whatever Zantha was...the television hadn't explained.

Echo continued to flip through the channels. Just as she was giving up hope of finding anything worthwhile to watch, she stumbled into a new program that was just beginning. She couldn't read the title, but it seemed to be something like "strange guy and I." What ever it was, it certainly the most entertaining program she'd found yet.

Fascinated, she watched as an apartment that could have been Alex's was transformed through the course of the hour, with the help of several men who behaved very strangely. From their gestures and speech, she would have guessed them to be lovers of men rather than women. The man whose apartment they were fixing up was more like Alex. He claimed to be interested in making his place livable for his lady friend.

Livable seemed to mean new wall colors, flooring, furniture, and a lot less clutter. Echo took a serious look around Alex's place. It could stand to be made livable.

While several of the strange men spent time cleaning the bathroom and kitchen, another took the man shopping for new clothes. Echo liked the garments they purchased. The green knitted shirt in particular would look very nice on Alex. After the shopping trip, one of the men who seemed to be a cook explained how to create a Greek dish with grape leaves and rice. It looked delicious and Echo realized that she was hungry.

Leaving the television playing, Echo explored the kitchen. The large white box held cold food, but outside of a bag of small orange vegetables, nothing she found interested her.

Where did food come from in this world? Obviously Alex didn't grow it himself...he had no garden that she knew of. Perhaps there was a market nearby.

Grabbing a few of the orange vegetables, Echo returned to the living room and examined it carefully. While Alex had done some work clearing the floor and tables of trash, there was still a lot of clothing lying around.

She picked up one shirt and immediately regretted it. The distinct odor of Alex, while intoxicating in person and small amounts, overwhelmed her senses. She temporarily lost interest in her vegetarian lunch.

Perhaps she should wash some of his garments. That would at least be something to do. There were no streams around, but Alex had a bathing tub in his bathroom. She could use that.

Humming happily Echo began collecting items to wash.

Twenty minutes later she leaned back on her heels. Well, there was one problem with this idea…it was a lot of work! As a nymph Echo had never had more than one gown to deal with. Alex must own at least a dozen shirts and nearly that many pants. The bathing tub was filled and there was another basket filled, ready to be washed.

There must be an easier way, she decided. She left the clothes to soak and returned to the living room. A play was showing on the television. A woman and two men were arguing over a baby, and who'd fathered it. Echo took a close look at the child. It didn't really look like either of the prospective parents. The background music swelled and the scene changed to a woman with piles of dirty clothes, smiling as she pointed to a box and a large metal machine.

Fascinated, Echo watched as the clothes went into the machine. She crept closer to the television the woman poured powder from the box into the machine. Minutes later the same woman held up a basket filled with dry folded clothing. How clever…a washing machine!

That's what she needed. The trouble was, where to find one.

She tried to remember if she'd seen a washing machine in the apartment. Outside of a box in the kitchen that held a collection of dirty dishes, there was nothing like a clothes washer. There was a box of powder like the woman on the TV had used under the sink. There must be a machine nearby that Alex used.

Depressed, Echo settled onto the couch. Obviously she was supposed to have used a clothes washer for doing the laundry, but she hadn't. Instead she'd filled the bathtub and now had a bunch of wet clothes to deal with. There was probably a washer around somewhere, but it wasn't in the apartment.

Alex would be home in an hour and he wouldn't be happy to find his bathtub filled with wet clothes.

Echo felt like crying.

After a couple of tearful moments, she decided to change the channel on the television again. This was clearly the most important form of information in this time. Surely the magic television machine would be able to deliver to her something she could use to get herself out of this fix.

She picked a random set of numbers on the TV remote, hoping for the best.

Wow! Echo sat up and stared in amazement. Every part of the screen was filled with naked skin as men and women engaged each other in sex. Sex. Lots of sex. Sex with each other, sex with objects, sex between men and women, women and women, men and men.

It was a virtual cornucopia of sex.

Fate. It was clearly fate, telling her that no matter how much laundry she did, sex was what she needed to win a place with Alex.

The man could always hire someone else to do his laundry.

As she watched, the flurry of bodies sorted themselves out and she was able to make out individual couples and trios and—well—more than trios involved in prodding, licking, and groping each other. At the perimeter of the room was a single figure, not actively involved in the action, but watching, directing, and lending the occasional helping hand.

Echo stared at the woman, recognition coming slowly. *Nemesis?* Could it really be her sister nymph from so long ago? What was she doing in the television box, and why was she in this sexual playground?

Even stranger, why did she have a large purple penis in her hand?

Still mulling over these questions, Echo almost missed the first faint tapping against the TV screen. Attention caught, she realized that Nemesis was now right behind the screen, tapping the glass with her purple plaything.

"Echo!" Nemesis's face turned up into a happy grin. "You're out of your statue!"

"Out of statue," she acknowledged. She still wasn't sure how happy she was about it.

"This is wonderful. How did you get out? How long will you be here?" From behind her an arm appeared, wrapping itself around her waist. A man's face showed up behind her head, whispering something into her ear. She turned to glare at him.

"I'm not interested in fucking you. You will let go of me *now*." There was a loud smacking sound as Nemesis used her purple penis as a bludgeon. The wayward face and hand disappeared immediately.

"Hold on, Echo. I'll have to transfer to where you are."

Moments later, Nemesis materialized in the middle of the living room. Echo fell into her arms and both had a crying and laughing jag.

It had been three thousand years since they'd been together. A few reunion tears were called for.

Finally, Nemesis pulled away, wiping her eyes. "It is so wonderful to see you. I've missed you, sister."

"Miss you, too, Nemesis." All nymphs were sisters to each other, but Nemesis had always been close to her.

"You should call me Nina, like everyone else. You can talk, too, not just repeat words!"

Echo shrugged. "Repeat still, sometimes. Talking getting easier."

"Oh, that's wonderful. How did it happen?"

In her halting speech, Echo described how Alex had made love to her while she was solid, and how Aphrodite had broken the spell as a result.

"So this is his place?" Nina looked around with obvious disdain. "It's kind of a dump."

Echo felt compelled to defend Alex's home. "Not so bad. Needs cleaning. No housekeeper."

"No housekeeper, yeah, I can see that. Couldn't you have gotten seduced by someone rich—or at least a man who does his own laundry?"

"Laundry!" Echo suddenly remembered the clothes she'd left in the bathroom. She grabbed her sister's arm and pulled. "Need help!"

Nina took one look at the bathtub and broke into laughter. "I see you tried to make yourself useful."

"No washing machine," Echo tried to explain.

"Oh, I'm sure we can solve that. There is probably one in the building." Nina grinned at her. "Let's see if we can find it."

Moments later they were out of the apartment, damp clothes in arms. With an uncanny instinct Nina led the way to a basement laundry room. Once there she helped

Echo load the machine, reading the instructions on the lid for her.

Echo sighed. One thing about it—to get along in this world she needed to learn to read.

"All we need now is some money." Nina snapped her finger over her palm and a pile of silver coins appeared. She handed the bounty over to Echo.

Using the coins, Echo started the machine, carefully tucking the rest into the pocket of her t-shirt.

Over the sound of water filling the tub, Nina said, "Don't worry, you'll figure out how to make money like that soon."

"Can't…no magic…human now."

"*What!*" Nina stared in horror. "That man made you a mortal? Echo, that's terrible."

"Not his fault…Aphrodite…"

Nina grimaced. "Oh. I might have known. Our fair goddess is always having some kind of fun. Making you mortal for sleeping with a mortal is probably her idea of a good joke." She patted her sister's arm. "I'll ask around and see if I can't find a way to reverse it."

The machine whirred to life. Anxious to see what it was doing, Echo carefully lifted the lid. The movement stopped, but the clothes were still agitating in the soapy water. There really were simpler ways to do things here. With a machine like that, having a lot of clothes wouldn't be much trouble at all.

Why, she could have a different dress for every day of the week. Echo looked down at the borrowed t-shirt and shorts. They weren't really ugly, but she could go for having something new and pretty to wear. She hadn't wanted to put back on the gown she'd come to life in…it was attractive but she'd been wearing it for centuries!

She glanced over to find Nina giving her outfit a similar examination. "If you're going to be here a while, maybe we should do some shopping."

Alex hadn't wanted her to leave the apartment. "Should stay here," she said reluctantly. "No money."

Nina grinned at her and flicked her fingers again to show an oblong piece of plastic with raised letters. "No problem, sweetie. This trip will be on me. We'll call it a welcome to the world present."

Four hours later, Echo happily explored how to make the stove work, intent on making the rice and grape-leaf dish she'd learned about on the strange guy show. In addition to buying clothes, she'd talked Nina into stopping at a food market where Nina's "credit card" had purchased food as well as other necessities.

Her newly acquired humanity had needs, ones she'd solved in the pharmacy and feminine hygiene aisles. Thank the gods that Nina had been able to explain everything to her. While not troubled by such things herself, Nemesis knew a number of mortals and their problems and knew how to create a valid-looking prescription.

Pills for preventing pregnancy were a wonderful invention.

Having finished the laundry, which was now put away in the bedroom, Echo had given up her t-shirt and shorts for a light yellow blouse made from a satiny smooth fabric while a moss-green skirt swirled around her ankles. New gold-colored sandals covered her feet.

Under her garments was to-die-for underwear in black lace. She couldn't wait to see Alex's face when he caught sight of them.

Speaking of which, he should be home pretty soon. Coaxing the flame up under the pot of cooking rice, she checked the rest of the room. While it didn't look like the "after" picture on the strange guy show, it certainly looked a lot better. All of the clothes were gone and the papers and books had been collected and placed on the bookshelves. Walls that had been dim and dingy now had a soft clean off-white to them and the carpeting was a clean tan shag.

In the kitchen the sink had been emptied of dishes and the counters and floor gleamed as a result of the afternoon's polishing.

Nina had insisted on helping out, using the magic Echo no longer had access to, which was the only reason the place could have been fixed up in the time they'd had. She'd wanted to stay and meet Alex, but Echo had decided that wasn't such a good idea. Meetings with Nemesis often hadn't gone well in the past.

Certainly Narcissus had had thousands of years to regret it.

The strange guy show had finished with a romantic dinner for two, including candles and wine. Nina had helped her find both at the store. She'd set the table with a small jar candle but had been unable to find stemmed glasses or fancy plates in Alex's cupboards. Small plain glasses stood by the simple place settings, but bathed in the warm candlelight, it still looked nice.

Now if only he thought so too.

Nervously Echo checked on dinner again. It was almost ready. Hopefully Alex would be home soon…

The key in the lock announced Alex's return.

Chapter Six

Dumbstruck, Alex stared at what had been his untidy sanctuary. Was it the same place? He resisted the urge to go back out into the hall and recheck the door number, just in case he'd somehow opened the wrong door. This had to be the right place. His key had worked for one thing.

The beaming presence of Echo standing behind the counter in the kitchen was even better proof that this was his home.

Trying not to gape, he stepped into the room and removed his coat, putting it and his camera cases on the table near the door. Smiling, Echo came forward and took the coat, moving it to a new set of hooks on the wall.

What a great idea! Since there wasn't a closet, it was an excellent place to put his stuff. Quickly Alex took advantage of it, hanging the bags he normally carried with him to and from class. When done, he turned to once again try to take in the modifications surrounding him.

Clean. That was the first thing he noticed, and it was orderly. No piles of papers on the tables, no laundry on the floor waiting to be done. The kitchen had been scrubbed and dishes washed and put away. It looked great, and even smelled wonderful, particularly with the aroma of dinner cooking.

Echo put her arms around his neck, temporarily distracting him. Alex gazed down into her beautiful face and shy smile.

"Welcome...home," she said in her halting voice.

"Hey, babe," he answered, meaning to question her about the changes she'd made. Then she kissed him and all other thoughts fled. By the time he could think again, he was sitting on the couch holding a glass of wine.

Not a wineglass, of course. One of the many things Melody had taken was all of the fancy glassware they'd bought together. For a moment Alex wondered why he hadn't simply purchased some inexpensive replacements. Had he been that intent on allowing Mel's actions to hurt him that he'd continued to live as she'd left him rather than taking simple steps to fix matters? It was an interesting question.

The tart-sweetness of the icy cold amber liquid tasted fine, even if it was served in an old jelly jar. He sipped appreciatively, watching Echo busy herself in the kitchen. Whatever dinner was, it smelled wonderful.

She was a minx who insisted on having her own way. Like the way she'd convinced him to share the bed with her. He had to admit, making love this morning was a lot more fun than trying to sleep with blue balls. And now, with the apartment looking so nice, and a good dinner...

Maybe having her around was going to be a lot better than he'd expected.

She finished her immediate task and joined him on the couch with her own wine. For a moment they both just sipped and relaxed.

Alex examined the outfit she wore. It was obviously new and looked expensive. "New threads?" he asked, pointing to her skirt.

"New...yes. Shopping."

"Shopping?" The word caught him off-guard and he almost choked on his wine. "Where'd you get the money?"

"Nemesis...took me. Paid."

Wait a minute...some guy took her out shopping? Alex most certainly didn't like that! "Who is this Nemesis?" The name sounded familiar, like something from one of the old Greek myths he'd read, trying to find out information about Echo. "I told you not to leave the apartment, how did you meet him?"

Echo seemed startled by his vehemence. "Not leave...well, not to meet." She struggled with her words. "Nina was on television. She came here."

Hold on...Nemesis was a Nina, a woman? And she was where? "Show me where you saw her."

Echo turned on the TV and flipped through the channels. *Well, at least she'd learned to master the remote.* The channel changing stopped and she pointed to the screen.

"Nina was there."

Alex's jaw dropped as he realized Echo had managed to find the twenty-four-hour pornography channel he subscribed to. Two hundred channels and she'd found this one. He watched the writhing bodies and Echo's bright-eyed interest uneasily. What must she think of him if she knew he watched this kind of stuff?

Taking the remote from her, he turned off the set.

"So you saw this Nina on this channel and then she came here. She's someone you know?"

Echo beamed at him. "My sister."

"Sister?" Echo's sister worked in porno films? Suppose she talked Echo into doing that kind of thing. He didn't want her involved in making sex films.

She nodded eagerly. "Nemesis is Nina and sister. Took me shopping. Food, clothes. Helped laundry, apartment." Echo shook her head and rose to return to the kitchen. "Needed so much."

"Laundry?" All of a sudden Alex realized how much had gotten done in the few hours he'd been gone. Echo and her sister had been very busy.

He was about to sit down to a good meal in a clean apartment with a beautiful woman wearing a lovely outfit, and for once he hadn't paid for any of it. So why didn't that feel as good as he thought it would? He'd always thought that having to spend money on Melody was why he'd gotten fed up with her.

When he'd taken Echo in, he'd expected to have to buy stuff for her and take care of her. Now with her sister's help it seemed like she was taking care of him and he wasn't sure he liked that.

He should have been the one to take Echo shopping and buy new clothes for her. She was so proud of the ones she was wearing, he could see it in the way she smoothed the fabric over her knees when she sat down, and the admiring glances she gave her sandal-clad feet. It would have been fun to watch her try clothes on.

As he thought about it, this was her first dinner since becoming human. He should have taken her out someplace nice, where they'd serve the wine in real glasses and where she wouldn't have needed to cook.

Alex felt unexpectedly disgruntled when Echo called him to the table.

* * * * *

What in Hades was wrong with Alex? Echo watched him eat his dinner as if each bite soured in his mouth. Was there something wrong with the food?

She took a big bite of the stuffed grape leaves. Delicious!

Her first real meal, alone with Alex. Did he have any idea how romantic this was? Maybe not. She took another glance at the way he scowled at his dinner and sighed.

How was she going to get him to love her? She knew he hadn't really wanted her here, but she expected him come around eventually. Still, it was getting awfully hard to wait for him to do so.

He hadn't even kissed her since the one by the door, nor thanked her for the work she'd done.

Maybe her new wardrobe would help. Nina had helped her pick out some very nice things.

It was funny thinking of Nemesis as Nina. Her sister had explained why she'd changed her name. Nemesis had become a word that meant one's worst enemy, just as her name meant a reflected sound.

In fact, Echo was thinking she should maybe do the same thing. But what kind of name could she pick?

She watched her silent dining companion with speculation. Maybe Alex would have some ideas.

"Name. Need new name," she said, pleased that the sentence she wanted came out almost the way she'd envisioned it.

"A new name? For you?"

"Like Nemesis is Nina. Echo not..." her voice trailed off, unsure of how to say what she wanted.

"Yeah, Echo is a kind of strange name for someone these days. Everyone would think it's a joke." Alex seemed to ponder the matter carefully. Suddenly he smiled and the change in his mood made the whole room seem brighter.

"Hey, I guess since I'm responsible for your becoming human, I get to pick a name for you." Alex thought for a moment. "There is one name I've always kind of liked...Chloe." He grinned. "It even has most of the same letters as your name."

Chloe? Echo turned the name around in her mind. She'd never heard it before, but she liked it. She particularly liked that Alex had picked it for her.

"Chloe," she said softly. It rolled gently off her tongue. "Nice."

"Yeah, it's a nice name. You want me to call you Chloe?"

She glanced down, suddenly feeling shy under his now friendly gaze. "Yes. Please."

"Okay, Chloe." He picked up another forkful of dinner, eating it with gusto. "This is pretty good. A kind of Greek dish isn't it?"

Chloe nodded, wondering what had changed. Why would a man be grumpy one minute and pleased the next? She watched as he dug into his meal, his whole mood changed. Maybe he'd just been hungry...sometimes that made a man cranky.

"Watched TV. Saw cook, clean."

"Yeah, babe. I noticed the cleaning part."

She looked up to see a sheepish grin on his face.

"The place looks great... I should have said something." Alex took a deep breath. "I'm not real good with words, babe. I don't know how to tell someone how I feel. You did an amazing job fixing up my apartment, and I appreciated dinner. Thank you."

Tentatively Chloe reached over and touched his hand. "Not good with words, either. Like to cook, clean. For you."

"For me?" He didn't seem to know how to take that. "I'm not used to that, either."

He fingered the fabric of her blouse. "This is nice."

"More nice...in bedroom."

"You have more new clothes? Like these?" At her nod, Alex leaned forward, an interested look in his eye. "Echo...I mean Chloe, would you mind posing for me? There's a photo project I need to do for my Master's thesis and you'd be a perfect subject."

She didn't know what a photo was, but she was happy to help. "Help, Alex? Yes. I'll help."

"Great!" Alex jumped up and went for the black cases he'd carried in. In moments he was setting up all sorts of equipment in the living room, long poles with lights on them and a three-legged stand with a small box on top. From the way he handled the small box, it was something very precious to him.

A small surge of jealousy slipped through her. Why would Alex find a box so much more exciting than she was? Well, at least he felt passion for something.

While he set up, Chloe cleared the table, rinsing the dishes. She'd yet to figure out how to operate the machine for dishwashing. Perhaps Alex would show her?

"Hey, babe, leave those. I'll get to them later. Right now I'd like to get some pictures of you."

Somehow she doubted Alex would really wash the dishes, but she was happy to move to the couch. As he directed, she sat up straight, one arm along the back of the couch, the other resting on her knee.

He held another box smaller than the one on the tripod. "This is a digital camera. I want to get some quick shots with it so I can see the results right away."

Holding it to his face, Alex pressed a button on top of the box. A bright light flashed, temporarily blinding her, and she heard a whirring sound.

As her vision cleared, she saw Alex examining the back of his box. A big grin broke out across his face. "Oh babe, you photograph even better than I expected." His big body exuded excitement as he held up the camera to her. "Take a look."

The back of the camera had a tiny screen, like that of the television. It showed a still picture of…why it was her! It was an instant picture of her, just as she'd seen herself in the mirror earlier. Her blonde hair cascaded down her shoulders framing a face dominated by green eyes wide with curiosity over what Alex was going to do.

"It's me."

"Yeah, it's you, babe, and you look great." He caressed her chin, holding it to turn her face into the light. For a moment Chloe wondered if he was going to kiss her. "You are so beautiful. Gorgeous body and a lovely face. You'd make a great model."

He let go of her chin and she fought her disappointment as he busied himself with the rest of the equipment. It wasn't quite a declaration of love, but she clearly had his interest. According to Nina, that was half the battle in getting a man to love her.

Now to fight the other half.

Alex turned on the standing lights and used his other camera to photograph her, the bigger one that wasn't digital. Occasionally he used the flash but mostly he didn't. The camera made a click and a whirring noise whenever he pushed the button. He positioned her a couple of times, sometimes having her lie on the couch, sometimes sitting. At one point he pulled the bottom of her skirt up to show more of her legs.

It grew hot under the lights, uncomfortably so. Not used to wearing so many clothes, Chloe unbuttoned the top of her blouse, trying to cool off.

She caught the flash of interest in Alex's eyes, and getting cooler stopped being the focus of removing her top. She unfastened another button and spread the opening of the fabric. Just the top of her breasts showed but she heard Alex's quick intake of breath.

He lifted the camera to his eye. *Click, whir.* "Oh babe. Yeah, like that."

Chloe smiled. *This could be fun.* She sat up and leaned against the back of the couch, letting the blouse gape open. A hint of her bra showed, black lace against her pale skin.

Click, whir, whir. Alex licked his lips and gave her a hungry smile. "More, babe. Show me more."

Happy to oblige, Chloe unbuttoned the last two buttons, letting the blouse gape further. *Click, whir, whir.* She opened the blouse, fanning herself slowly as if to cool down. Alex's eyes blazed and the heat from them scorched her bared skin.

Click, whir, whir, whir. "Okay, now take it off." Alex's voice sounded harsh and his breathing had picked up.

She did as he asked, letting the fabric caress her shoulders as it went, taking it slow. The softness teased her skin as it slid down her back. Involuntarily she arched her back, her breasts poking higher in the air. Her nipples pebbled prominently in their black lace holders.

"Oh, babe." *Click, whir, whir, whir, whirrrr.* "That is a nice bra you've got. What else do you have on?"

Hiding her smile, Chloe reached for the fastening of her skirt. Watching the anticipation in Alex's eyes, she tugged on it, pretending to have trouble with it. His breath stopped as she finally managed the button and zipper closure. Climbing onto her knees, she let the skirt slide down her hips, revealing the barely-there black lace panties that matched the bra.

The look in Alex's eyes turned predatory.

Click, whir, whirrrr, whirrrrr.

She dropped the skirt and blouse on the floor and stretched out on the couch, one leg bent. Leaning up on one arm she gave him a meaningful look.

Click, whiirrrrrrrrrrr. Alex put the camera down and moved to the couch. "Chloe, babe, I'm dying here."

Chloe stretched her arm and patted the now straining crotch of his pants. "Doesn't look dead."

With a groan Alex dropped to his knees and pulled her into his arms. "Nope, not dead, but it's going to be very busy making you come." He buried his head in her hair. "You look wonderful but you smell even better, babe."

He smelled pretty wonderful, too. Hands on his cheeks, she explored his mouth with her tongue. He tasted even better.

"Enough photos," she told him, hands still framing his face. "Make love."

Alex stood, Chloe cradled in his arms. "Yeah, babe. I like the way you think."

Chapter Seven

Placed in the middle of the bed, Echo turned to unfasten Alex's pants, setting free his engorged cock, proud and ready. It was a magnificent sight. If she'd wondered before about his wanting her, he most certainly wanted her now.

She closed her mouth over the plum-shaped purple tip. He tasted just as good tonight as he had this morning. Swirling her tongue over the narrow opening at the top, she picked up droplets of his sweet pre-cum. Alex groaned and slipped his fingers into her hair, urging her to take him deeper in her mouth.

Enthusiastically, Chloe complied with his unspoken request. Impossible as it seemed, his cock grew larger in her mouth, filling it even as she took as much of him as she could. He whispered instructions, then approval. Finally all he could manage were low moans of delight.

A shiver ran through him and he seized her shoulders, pulling her away. Wordless, he stared down at her, his eyes blazing with passion.

"I'm not ready to finish quite yet," Alex told her when he regained his ability to speak. "And when I do finish, I want you screaming along with me."

He pulled his shirt off over his head, the black t-shirt flying to the corner. Again Chloe enjoyed the view of his smooth chest and the sprinkling of fine hair that covered it. Since he wouldn't let her lick his cock anymore, she contented herself with teasing his flat male nipples into erections of their own. Against her belly his cock felt solid and ready.

Alex pulled her up by the elbows, kissing her hard. "The things you do to me, babe. Let me finish getting undressed, please?"

Grinning, she settled back on her heels while he untied his shoes and removed the rest of his clothing. Finally naked, Alex moved onto the bed and approached her, hands outstretched to capture her in his arms. Willingly she let him take hold of her waist, rubbing his hands across her flesh to slide under the black lace underwear Nina had talked her into this afternoon. After a lifetime of being bare under her clothing, it had been difficult to see the need for panties and a bra.

"If there's one thing a man likes," her sister had told her, "it's seeing a woman decked out in lace. Makes him think about how much fun it will be to get her out of it."

Alex's face told her how right Nina had been. Chloe giggled. These weren't even the most interesting set of underwear she'd gotten.

"You look so good, babe. Like a Christmas present all wrapped up."

She patted his chest. "Present for you."

"Yeah, for me." He grinned at her, all admiration in his face. "The apartment was one thing, and dinner was another. All great, I should say. But seeing you like this, that's the best present of all." He tilted her face to his. "You're one in a million, babe."

It wasn't a declaration of love, but she wouldn't bother about that for now. So long as she was welcome in his bed and his home, she'd find a way to make him love her. That was the deal, and she'd manage it.

She caught his face in her hands, letting her fingers stroke his cheeks. His unshaved beard was harsh against her palms. "Want you, Alex."

"Me too, babe."

He moved to kiss her mouth, hands moving to unfasten her bra and toss it aside. Freed, her breasts fell into his hands, and he kneaded them, his fingers finding her nipples. He twisted them lightly, sending electric shocks down her belly. His tongue engaged hers as he fondled her breasts, a passionate game of distraction. Which part of her could he make sense more, her nipples or her mouth?

Involved in the game, she missed it when one hand slipped off her breast and headed for her underpants. She only noticed when he peeled away the covering to find her hidden clit and caress it. The pressure there made all other sensations fly away.

"Alex!" Chloe moaned under his gentle assault, widening her knees to give him better access.

He smiled, skimming her underwear down her thighs to toss them away. "This is one time when the present is far better than the packaging." Pushing her back onto the pillows, he spread her legs. Settling between her thighs, Alex grinned up at her across her stomach. "Last night you used your mouth to turn me into Jell-o. Now it's my turn." He leaned forward to lick her folds.

She wasn't sure what Jell-o was, but it must be something that quivered and shook because that's what Chloe did for the next several minutes. Sensation after sensation arrowed from what Alex had called her pussy as he licked, sucked, and blew on her most sensitive spots. Of all things Alex had done to her, this was the most intimate, his pleasuring her with his tongue and lips. What's more, he seemed to like it. In the rare moments when she wasn't shuddering, overcome with the amazing feelings he was driving through her, she could see his smile, the pleasure in his eyes at her cries.

He liked doing this to her. Alex enjoyed making her come with just the actions of his mouth and she loved every moment of it. If she wasn't careful, Alex wouldn't be the only one losing his heart...Chloe sensed some serious danger to her own. At the moment she didn't care at all. Later she'd worry. Right now she had better things to think about.

The next oncoming orgasm for instance...that was a much bigger worry.

Finally she could take no more. She needed more than his tongue in her slit. Fun as this was, she needed something a lot bigger and harder inside her. Chloe tugged on Alex's hair until she pulled his attention from her clit.

"Please..."

Alex grinned. "Please what?"

She licked her lips. "Please, now."

The grin turned mischievous. "What do you want, Chloe? Say the words."

"I want...you..."

"And what do you want me to do?"

Oh, the man was impossible. He knew just what she wanted but obviously he'd decided to make her tell him. Such a wonderful time for a language lesson...*not*! She'd have to say it, find the words. Very well, what was that expression that Nina had used?

"Fuck me, Alex!"

He rose from between her legs, his grin as broad as his cock was thick. "Oh, babe. I thought you'd never ask."

Instantly he fitted his broad length to her pussy, driving home with a single slow stroke. Chloe shuddered as he claimed her. It seemed like it took forever for him to completely enter her and then he stopped as soon as he was completely encased.

Alex gazed down at her. "Babe, I hope you're ready for a wild ride. I don't think I'm going to make it last too long tonight."

She was ready for anything...or at least that's what she told herself as he pulled back then pushed home again. In and out, then again. Such a simple thing to do, but each stroke woke another fire in her until she felt aflame. Burning love, that's what this was, and she was tinder under him, his cock the match.

But Alex wasn't immune to the heat between them. His face reddened as he stroked deep within her, and perspiration beaded on his brow. Chloe slid her hands down his back and felt them dampen as his skin became slick with sweat.

Inside her the flame took hold and she cried out once, then twice at the glorious torment. Alex stiffened and jerked, coming to a sudden halt. Arms shaking he stared down at her. Chloe whimpered at the interruption

"Babe, this is it. Can't wait longer."

"No talk, Alex. Fuck me."

Groaning, he took up his rhythm again, but only for a moment before finishing with a loud yell. His last drive pushed Chloe into one last flaming climax that wiped away all her recollections of previous orgasms. For one brief moment she felt as the phoenix bird must feel, on turning to flame.

What seemed like hours later, she returned to herself to find Alex sprawled across her. She kissed his skin and tasted his salty sweat. Raising himself onto his elbow, he stared down into her face.

"God, Echo. That was fantastic."

"Chloe. Call me Chloe."

"Oh, yeah. Sorry, I forgot." He settled himself beside her, one arm behind her back. "I thought it was great before, but tonight was even better."

"Better sex? Like making love?"

Something in his face changed, became guarded. "I guess that might be it. We know each other better and that changes things."

Alex seemed to pull away from her after that. Chloe tried not to feel the hurt as he pulled his arm away and put distance between them on the bed. He glanced over at the clock and grimaced. "I've got to get ready to work, Chloe. I'm doing graveyard shift at the museum again tonight."

Moments later she heard the shower as Alex prepared to leave her again, this time to go to his job. This was going to be her life with him, watching him leave for class or to go to work. She'd stay here, keeping his home nice until he returned to her.

Keeping his bed warm until he returned to it to make love to her.

Chloe sat up and pulled on the new robe she'd bought today. Was that what she wanted, to stay home while Alex left to do the things he wanted in the outside world? So far she hadn't minded, but then she'd only been here the one day, and she'd spent part of that with Nina.

There had to be more for her to do than simply keep house for Alex.

Alex appeared in the doorway of the bathroom, hair damp from the shower, a towel draped over his hips. Chloe admired the lines of his body as he moved around the room, getting underwear from a drawer, clothes from his closet.

Buttoning his uniform shirt, he paused to smile at her and her heart tripped. "It sure is nice having clean clothes to wear. It'll be nice to have someone to come home to, too."

After tying his shoes he came over to sit on the bed next to her, and kissed her gently on the mouth. "Go ahead and get some rest and I'll see you in the morning."

After he'd gone, Chloe climbed out of bed to go to the kitchen. As she'd predicted, the dinner dishes hadn't magically washed themselves. For a moment she missed her own magic. Several times today it would have been nice to flick her fingers and have items clean themselves.

Sighing, she filled the sink with water and soap and set about washing up the hard way. The job required little of her attention and her thoughts returned to her earlier questions.

Assuming she could win Alex's love so she could stay in this body, would that really be enough? Sure, sex would be great and having his company would be fine, but what else would there be for her to do?

The apartment was clean, at least temporarily, and the clothes were washed. She had food in the house for the next few days. She looked around the living room. So bare.

Spartan, and she'd never been fond of Sparta's style of decorating. Too austere for her tastes.

There was so much to buy. Wineglasses, new bed linens. Some nice dishes, maybe some decorative items.

Chloe thought about it. She needed to shop, but that took money, or at least credit cards like the one Nina had used. Alex had a couple of the plastic sheets; she'd seen them in his wallet. Maybe she could take one in the morning and borrow it for the day.

Sitting on the couch she grinned. This was a great idea, to fix up Alex's house for him. He'd enjoyed her cleaning it, he'd be happy to have it look nicer. She wouldn't tell him, though. She'd have everything done by the time he got home tomorrow evening and surprise him.

Chapter Eight

Alex hesitated in the hall outside the door to his apartment. What had Echo been up to today? When he'd asked this morning before heading for school, she'd been somewhat mysterious about her plans for the day. She'd hinted that he might be coming home to a surprise.

For a moment he imagined her on the other side of the door, wearing high-heels, an apron, and nothing else. He grinned at the mental image, adding a pair of martini glasses, one in each hand. Now that would be a great surprise!

Slipping the key in the lock, he opened the door.

Oh. Dear. God. Alex stared at his apartment, which had now been taken over by the kitsch fairies.

Bric-a-brac, figurines, knick-knacks, and assorted other crap covered every horizontal surface of the room. Statues of horses, of fairies, and of cupids with dainty wings. Miniature statues of animals, owls, and bears. Even a Greek goddess or two.

It looked like his grandmother's home. No, wait. His grandmother had better taste than this.

Alex closed his eyes and reopened them. It didn't help, the stuff was still there.

Echo emerged from the kitchen, holding a wineglass. "Surprise!"

Yeah, he was surprised all right. "Where…" his voice caught for a moment. Trying again, Alex managed to finish the sentence. "Where did all this come from?"

She beamed. "Shopping!" Echo looked about, her attitude intense satisfaction. "Went shopping. Decorate."

"With your sister? She let you buy all this stuff?"

Echo shook her head. "No. I buy."

"Where did you get the money?"

Some of Echo's exuberance faded. "Uh. Credit card."

A sinking feeling hit the pit of Alex's stomach. "Whose credit card, Echo?"

Now she was distinctly uncomfortable looking. "Yours. Borrow. Not okay?"

Alex pulled his wallet out of his pants and searched through it. Sure enough, his one and only credit card was gone. The sinking feeling turned into outright fury. She'd taken his card, stolen it and used it to buy a lot of junk.

He held out his hand. "Give it back, Echo. And I want the receipts, too."

Her eyes widened. "Receipt? What mean?"

"The pieces of paper you got when you bought this junk. I want them, now!"

Her lower lip trembling, Echo scrambled back to the bedroom and returned with a handful of paper, his plastic card on top. She offered it to him, flinching when he grabbed them from her hand.

He added up the numbers. Fifty-three dollars from one store, one hundred twenty-five from another. Three thirty-one, four twenty-four…nearly a thousand dollars spent in one day. In addition to the decorative shit that littered his living room, there were bed linens, dishes, and stemware.

One thousand dollars. It was more than he'd managed to save, more than what was in the bank at the moment, all the ready cash he had in the world.

Alex staggered over to the couch and sat, thin sheets clutched tight in his hand. He'd skimped and saved, struggled to keep expenses down, and in one day Echo had spent more than he'd managed to accumulate. Fury filled him, his free hand opening and closing in the air.

Echo had taken his credit card while he slept and used it to go "shopping". How could he have been so stupid? Why had he let his guard down around her? She was no better than Melody, taking advantage of him, taking his money.

She didn't even realize what she'd done was wrong. He watched the way she clutched her hands together and her dawning worry. She was just now figuring out she'd angered him.

"Not like, Alex?" She waved her arm around. "Not good?"

"Not good, Echo. Not at all good. Very bad." He shook the credit card slips under her nose. "I don't have the money to pay for all this. You spent too much. Way too much, and you spent it on stuff we don't need. How could you be this irresponsible?"

She turned from him and stepped away. Her shoulders shook with suppressed grief and he didn't have the heart to yell at her further. What was the use? She hadn't realized what she was doing was wrong.

Alex sank further onto the couch. "What am I going to do? I'll have to work more. Take on more hours. Or sell something." His shoulders slumped. "Maybe one of my cameras. I could raise some money there."

"What?" Echo sat up and stared at him.

"I can't pay for this stuff, Echo. I don't have that much in savings. I'll need to do something to raise some cash."

"Not sell camera." Echo stood before him, eyes wide, her lower lip trembling. "My mistake, I pay." She grabbed his hand, and he felt something fall into his palm. She closed his fingers over it and stepped back.

Opening his hand he found a pair of earrings, two slender loops with tiny stars and a crescent moon dangling from them.

Echo backed away from him, gaze locked on the floor. She sat on one of the dining chairs, her shoulders hunched forward over the table. One hand reached up to stroke her empty earlobes and she shuddered. Her head dropped into her hands and she shook with sobs.

Alex looked down at his hand. Her earrings. She'd given him her earrings to sell, to pay for her mistake. He examined them closely. They were beautiful things, with wonderful workmanship. *Probably made by some mythical god.* They looked old, even though they were in perfect shape. He guessed they were worth several hundred, at the very least. He looked back at Echo, crying into her hands.

They were worth far more than that to her. They were all she had. The only things she owned.

Alex took one deep breath, then another. This wasn't something that Melody would have done. No matter what his ex had done, she'd never offered to pay for a mistake. She'd never given up anything she considered hers for any reason.

Echo had.

He picked up the nearest piece of statuary, noting the small tag on the bottom. He checked another, then another. Finally he stood beside Echo and tapped her on the shoulder. She raised her tear-soaked face to his.

Some women looked good when they cried. Melody, for instance, on the rare times he'd seen her in tears, had had a noble cast to her face even with thin streams of tears flowing from her eyes. She'd had the look of a martyr then.

Echo did not look good in tears. Her eyes turned red and her nose ran. Deep heavy sobs made it hard for her to breath and she gasped like a fish out of water. Suppressing his smile, Alex pulled a handkerchief from his pocket. A clean handkerchief, he realized—clean because she'd done his laundry.

He handed it to her. "Dry your eyes, Echo."

She wiped her face, blowing her nose in the thin fabric. There was still a woeful look on her face when she finished. "Sorry, Alex. So sorry."

"I know, babe. You only wanted to make the place look nice. Here, put them back in your ears." He handed her the earrings. Confusion showed in her eyes as she replaced the thin loops through her earlobes. He heard the soft jingle of the tiny bits of metal hitting each other.

"Not sell camera?" Her worried tone seemed plaintive.

Alex pulled her to her feet and gathered her into his arms. He rubbed her tense back reassuringly. "That shouldn't be necessary. Most this stuff still has a price tag. We'll pack it up and return it tomorrow. The stuff we need to keep, I've got the money for. We'll be all right. Just don't do it again. If you need to buy something, you check with me first."

The tension eased from her body and she leaned into his arms. "Promise, Alex. Promise."

* * * * *

They spent the rest of the evening packing up the items she'd bought. Most of it had been returnable. Echo hadn't been inclined to argue about it as he'd put everything back into the boxes, even the wonderful little horse statue she'd found.

He was right. It was his money and she had no business spending it without his knowledge, so she'd bitten her lip as the precious little figurine had been wrapped up with the rest.

She didn't complain at all, even when he insisted that the new dishes and stemware go back. Those weren't really luxuries, but he insisted cheaper versions could be found.

After Alex left for work, Echo returned to the kitchen to wash the dinner dishes. One hand kept straying to her ears, to fondle the tiny stars and moon. Praise the gods he hadn't kept her earrings. They'd been a gift from the goddess Artemis herself, and she'd hated to part with them, but it hadn't been fair that Alex sacrifice one of his cameras for her folly.

It had been folly, to spend so much on things they didn't need. She'd so enjoyed shopping that she hadn't realized how much she was spending. Bare and empty as Alex's home was, she didn't need to fill it with beauty to make it livable. All she really needed was him...to love her, of course.

It would be nice to have a little beauty around, and there were things she needed that she didn't want to ask Alex for. Yesterday she'd been able to use Nina's credit cards, but something about the way Alex had reacted to her sister's generosity told her that relying on Nina wouldn't be much appreciated.

Men hadn't changed that much over the centuries. A man still liked to provide for what he felt was his.

That gave Chloe a warm glow. Alex already regarded her as his...certainly that had to be a step towards love.

Finished with the dishes, Chloe looked around the apartment. It needed more work, but she wouldn't try to furnish it with Alex's card again. Unless she could get the strange guys from the television to come in, fixing up Alex's home would take money. Nina had given her a small amount of cash so that she wouldn't be entirely dependent on him, but she needed to save that for emergencies.

Alex worked as a museum guard for money. Maybe she could get a job, too? But doing what?

Still not tired, Chloe turned on the TV and flipped through the channels. The sex program came on, but Nina wasn't there so Chloe moved on. That's how Nina earned her money, working on shows like that. Maybe her sister could get her a job...

No. If she wanted Alex to love her, she'd have to avoid sex with other people. A man who didn't want her taking money from others certainly wouldn't want her having sex with someone else. Besides, the idea of being intimate with anyone other than Alex really didn't appeal to her.

Another cooking show came on, this time one with two chefs battling to see who could create the best meals. Fascinated, Chloe sat to watch.

If only she could learn to cook like that.

Well, why not? She'd certainly mastered the dishes she'd made last night and tonight. Chloe observed the techniques the men used. It didn't seem that difficult and the results were spectacular. Maybe if she learned to cook really well, she could get a job in a restaurant like the one Nina had taken her to yesterday for lunch.

Her eye fell on the syllabus from the university Alex attended. After her failure to understand the directions on the washer in the basement, it had become clear that the first thing Chloe had needed was to learn how to read. During their day together Nina had solved that problem by using a little of her magic to gift Chloe with the ability to understand written English. They'd used the class listings and television guide as practice.

Picking up the course book, she turned to the section on culinary arts, noting that there was a beginner's class with a session starting tomorrow afternoon, while Alex would be at the university. Going to class would give her something to do and keep her from shopping.

All she needed to do was show up and register. Chloe grinned. This was definitely something she could do.

Chapter Nine

Two weeks later, Chloe sat on the couch in the mid-afternoon, planning her trip to the grocery for the next day. After some negotiating with Alex, promising that there'd be no repeat of her first solo shopping excursion, she'd wrangled a budget from him to buy food and necessities. After all, she'd argued, he'd spent the same amount on take-out food as she needed to run the household.

At first he'd seemed reluctant to give her money, doling it out a few dollars at a time. But when she'd managed to not spend more than he'd given her for several days running, he'd given her a full week's allowance at a time.

That felt good, that she'd proved herself to him.

By careful management she'd stretched the money such that she'd been able to buy some inexpensive but nice dishes to replace the plastic plates they'd been using and a set of silverware where all the pieces matched. They even had new glassware, including a pair of real wineglasses.

None of it had cost much. Chloe had discovered the discount store and its periodic sales. She'd been a little surprised that simple household budgeting had come so easy for her. After all, there was very little call for a wood nymph to handle money. But one of the earliest lessons in her cooking classes had involved managing the books for a restaurant kitchen. Both a household and a restaurant had similar needs for handling expenses.

Even her professor had been impressed. He'd given her extra credit for several ideas she'd had about bargain hunting and wholesale prices on food and tableware. He'd told her she had the makings of a fine restauranteur. Unused to having someone praise her mental abilities, Chloe had been pleased at the man's praise, telling Alex all about it that evening over dinner. While Alex hadn't said much, he had seemed proud of her accomplishments.

Or maybe he was just happy he wouldn't be stuck taking care of her forever. Since starting the class, Chloe knew she'd be able to make it on her own without him, once she'd gotten him to admit to loving her. She could leave then.

Trouble was, she wasn't sure she wanted to be without him and leaving wasn't something she could even imagine.

Their weekdays together had become something of a routine. Alex worked night guard duty at the museum from eleven until six. He'd come home and join her in bed for a few hours...some of which were spent sleeping. Then he'd drive them to the university for their classes in the afternoon. When he had a class that went later than hers she took the public bus home, sometimes stopping in town at the grocery. Alex's apartment was near enough that she could walk from there.

She loved the little city they lived in. It was small enough that someone used to walking—like her—could get almost anywhere without a car. The bus ran often enough that she took it when she needed to go someplace further away, like the university.

Once she was home, she would clean or cook, and sometimes watch television—to improve her English, she'd told Alex, but the truth was she enjoyed the silly and strange stories available there.

She always cooked dinner and they'd eat together, then Alex would sometimes get out his cameras and photograph her. That often led to them making love before he left for his job.

That was the one disappointment for her. They rarely got to stay in bed together. Seven nights a week he worked. Sometimes he talked about when he'd be able to quit working at the museum, after he got his big break as a photographer.

Chloe secretly hoped she could find a job before then so that he could concentrate on school and not work every night. She'd investigated and found out that even an assistant chef made as much as a museum guard.

Of course, all this depended on her earning Alex's love.

Chloe sighed and put away her grocery list. She'd finish it later, after Alex left for work. Turning on the television, she tried to lose herself in a show about interior decorating. It was so different in this time than the one she'd last lived in. Such an array of colors and fabrics available and sometimes for such modest prices.

A commercial came on about a furniture store downtown. *It was having a sale on couches.* Chloe admired the clean lines of one with green leather upholstery.

That would look so good in her living room.

Quickly she caught herself. She meant Alex's living room, of course, and it was far too much money for now. This was getting serious. Now she was decorating the man's place as if she planned on being a permanent occupant.

How did one go about getting a man's love? Cooking wasn't doing it, nor was keeping the apartment clean. Sexy underwear had made his cock hard, but his heart hadn't softened towards her.

Their sex was great, but no matter what she did, he still kept control. He never called her anything but Babe, or Honey. He rarely even used her name. The man said he'd never had better sex than what was between them but he didn't act like it meant anything to him.

Resting her chin on one hand, she flipped through the channels again, looking for her sister's sex program. Several times when she'd needed to talk to Nina, she'd been able to find her this way.

Maybe Nina would have some suggestions on driving a man wild in bed.

* * * * *

Chloe stared at the array of items on her bed, the result of her sister's ransacking the TV studio's prop department. Nina grinned at her as she lifted one item after the other in total bemusement. She had no idea what some of these things were even meant to do. As she examined each, she wondered what body parts they'd been used on before.

"Don't worry about this stuff," Nina said, "it's all right out of the box. We did a show on toys some time ago. They were donated by an online company I'd been working with so I got to keep everything we didn't find a home for."

One little item was shaped like a bunny with a long cord attached to a box that held batteries. She pressed the button and the bunny skittered around on the comforter top.

Nina's grin grew bigger. "It's a funny bunny vibrator. So small it will fit into the narrowest crack or crevice but delivers a real wallop to the nerve endings."

Chloe stared at her sister. "What kind of crevice?"

"Oh the usual ones…guys like that sort of thing."

Chloe wasn't so sure Alex would enjoy something shoved into any of his cracks. Of course she could be wrong…

"Does he like to take baths with you? Here's a vibrating rubber duck. Or maybe a dolphin? These little babies work underwater."

Chloe laughed. "Do you have something less obvious in shape? Alex isn't much of an animal lover."

Nina grabbed another item, which looked like some sort of sculpture, all points and knobs of clear plastic. She flicked the switch at the bottom and held it against Chloe's hand. It hummed and tingled across her skin.

Chloe smiled "I might want to keep that one for when Alex isn't around."

"It's yours then," Nina handed the toy over with a flourish. "Of course this isn't answering what you need in the driving-a-man-wild department."

Chloe stared at the other offerings on the bed. One was a package that had a collection of items, including a video, book, what looked like a belt, and a long, heavy replica of a man's erect cock.

She pointed to it. "What is this?"

Nina picked it up and chuckled wickedly. "This is a kit for couples. It's called 'Spread 'em wide, Lover-boy'."

She placed it to one side. "No offense, Chloe, but I think that might be something more to my taste than yours."

"What are these for?" Chloe picked up a pair of what might be bracelets, except that they had a narrow chain connecting them.

"Those are some of the finest bondage handcuffs ever made. Perfect for a little master-slave action." Nina pointed to the interior of each circlet with pride. "Notice how there's rubber inside. That cushions the cuff against the skin so it doesn't do too much damage when the slave gets to struggling...which they inevitably do."

"Slave? Master?"

"It's a game, Chloe. You take turns being in control, sometimes you're the master and sometimes he is. The other person is the slave and gets tied up."

She shrugged. "Some folks today call the master the 'top' and the slave the 'bottom', but I'm a bit old-fashioned."

Alex was already the top most of the time. He was so strong that anything he wanted to do he simply did. How could she persuade him to play the role of the bottom? "Why would someone want to be a slave?"

Nina locked her hands together, obviously pleased with her role as instructor. "What being a slave does is make it possible for someone to give in to not having control. You fasten their arms to the bed and they can't resist anything you do to them."

"A man gives up control? Just by being handcuffed?"

"Sure. They use these things in law-enforcement to control prisoners. Of course those cuffs don't have the rubber."

Chloe smiled. She'd wanted Alex to give up control for a short time while making love. This could be just the thing she was looking for!

"So why would a slave struggle if they've given up control?"

Nina held up a couple of items, one a small rod with feathers on the tip, and the other a longer rod with several thin leather straps. "Because nobody can resist struggling when you tickle them with these little items. Both heighten the sensations of where and how you touch them." She grinned. "I find guys really like this kind of thing."

"Really?" Chloe took the feather-topped toy and ran it across the back of her hand. It felt heavenly.

Nina slapped the leather straps across her hand. "Mind though, you have to have a safe word. If he's had enough he can use it and you stop."

Collecting the handcuffs, feather tickler, and mini-whip, Chloe nodded fervently. "Of course, I'll stop if he says the safe word."

She'll make the safe word something easy to remember. Like "love".

Chapter Ten

Something was definitely up. Chloe had looked like a cat who'd been into the cream all through dinner. Alex wasn't sure what the story was, but her eyes were brighter and her smile more satisfied than he'd seen in days.

Outside of bed, that is. She always looked satisfied when he got through with her.

Since she'd come to live with him, he'd felt like a cat in the cream, too. Food was great, apartment clean, clothes were washed…and the sex was great. He couldn't remember being happier, not even in the early days when Melody had been around. Of course, he remembered how that had panned out. Bad, real bad.

Good thing Chloe behaved nothing like Melody had. She didn't ask for anything, outside of money to get food. There were no trips to the mall or manicurist. She'd never had that gorgeous head of hers in a beauty salon.

Not that Chloe needed to go to a beauty salon. If she got any lovelier he'd probably stop breathing when he looked at her.

She'd even paid for her own classes, saying she had some money from her sister. Yep, Chloe was a very self-sufficient woman.

Maybe a little too self-sufficient. Outside of the bedroom she didn't ask him to do anything but give her the housekeeping money. He just wasn't used to a woman who didn't beg or plead for something. Melody had really spoiled him on women.

And not in a good way.

"Would you like more bread?" The look on Chloe's face was pure innocence, a sure sign she was up to something. He took a piece. Excellent, as always. Probably home-baked today.

"What did you do this afternoon?" He asked the question casually, as if the answer didn't matter to him.

"Oh, this and that. Baked some bread."

He'd guessed that. She knew that he loved home-baked bread. She'd probably made it just to put him in a good mood. It was working because he was in a good mood, maybe in part because she was.

But something was definitely up.

"Anything else?"

She shrugged. "My sister came to visit."

Oh, oh. He'd better keep this casual. He didn't trust the infamous Nina. "That's nice. When are you going to let me meet her?"

"Oh, sometime," Chloe said vaguely. "She gave me something I'd like to show you — later."

Later? The hackles on the back of his neck went up with suspicion. Alex took another piece of bread and chewed it slowly.

Chloe winked at him. *Chloe winked at him — that wasn't like her!* Alex tried to relax. Maybe it was just another set of fancy underwear. Nothing wrong with that. One thing Nina had excellent taste in was underwear.

He forced a smile at her. "I'll look forward to it."

* * * * *

Alex was still forcing his smile two hours later, after he'd gotten the best photos to date of Chloe. He put away the camera while Chloe finished up the dishes and headed for the bedroom.

Everything in her attitude told him that something was still very much up...but she'd been totally responsive during their photo shoot and he'd done close to a week's work just in the few hours.

His portfolio was shaping up nicely. He needed some outdoor shots still. Maybe he and Chloe could head out to the country this weekend and he'd photograph her there. It was too bad it was winter. He could just imagine her under a tree, wearing just a thin garment, all that creamy skin of hers contrasting with the green grass. Maybe some flowers in the right places giving her modesty. He was going for artistic shots of her, not porn.

She'd seen some of his pictures and had been nothing but complimentary, not minding at all the occasional bare breast or ass shot. She'd never learned to be embarrassed by her body — one of the reasons she was such an excellent model.

Her praise had made him feel better than that of his senior professor, who'd also exclaimed enthusiastically over his photos, saying if Alex kept this quality of work up, he'd be sure to get one of the positions he was applying for.

His professor has also asked pointed questions about Alex's model, probably wanting to hire her himself, and had been disappointed when Alex had told him it was his girlfriend and she didn't model professionally.

Not that she couldn't be a model, but Alex didn't like the idea of another man photographing Chloe. She was...his...well, girlfriend said it close enough for now. Anyway, she wanted to be a professional cook and that was fine with him.

"Alex, could I talk to you a moment?"

Something in her tone was warm and inviting. A grin crossed his face as he headed for the bedroom. Maybe now he'd find out what she'd been so secretive about.

He stepped through the door before he realized that the lights were out. Instead he saw lit candles by the down-turned bed, casting a warm, romantic glow. *Nice!* He'd always been a sucker for good lighting.

Alex stepped further into the room, expecting to see Chloe near the bed. Instead she came up from behind the door and snapped something down on his wrist.

"Hey! What's this?" Alex tugged on the narrow circlet locked tight around his wrist. A second one dangled from the short chain that attached them. Alex stared at the pair. *Handcuffs?*

Chloe danced to a few feet away and turned to grin at him. She was wearing some sort of little black lace teddy that pushed up her breasts and outlined her pubic triangle in an audacious display. Covering her long legs were black lace stockings held up by garters, and her feet wore what had to be six-inch heels. Alex wondered how she could stay balanced in them.

She wielded what looked like a tiny whip and slapped it against the palm of her hand. It made a puny sound like a wet noodle on a kitchen counter.

"You are my prisoner!" she said and struck a pose like that of a dominatrix in a dirty movie, wide legs and penetrating stare. Then she giggled, spoiling the effect.

Alex didn't know whether to be angry over her subterfuge or to burst out laughing. *A bondage game?* So this was what she'd been planning all afternoon. No doubt her sister, the porn queen, had put her up to it.

He glanced at the cuff on his arm, at her, and at the room. *Oh, what the hell*, she'd gone to so much trouble. He hadn't tried anything this kinky before, but how bad could it get? What was a little S&M between friends?

Besides, she looked absolutely hot in that get-up. His cock was already hard enough to pound nails at the thought of tearing it off her. If he were free to have his way, he'd have her sprawled on the bed before she could slap him with that dinky whip of hers. He'd shove himself inside her, and wham, bam it would be over in minutes. At least this way he might last a while.

Trying to control his snicker, Alex went down on one knee before Chloe's astonished face. "I am your servant, Mistress. What is your command?"

"Uh…" Chloe stared at him with wide eyes before pulling herself back into character. She gestured to his clothes with an imperious wave of her whip. "Remove those garments…*slave*."

He suppressed a chortle and went to work, removing his shoes, and socks, unbuttoning his shirt one button at a time. As he pulled his shirt off his shoulders he glanced over at "Mistress Chloe". She was looking more nervous that he'd seen in recent days, rolling the little whip around between her palms.

"You know," he said as he unfastened his pants, "If you get to be my mistress now, I get to play the master next time."

Her eyes fixed on his massive erection and she chewed on her lower lip. "No talking. We can discuss that later."

Smirking, Alex dropped his pants on the floor. "Just thought I'd mention it. I think I might enjoy having a little sex slave like you." The single cuff dangled from his wrist, the only thing left he wore. Naked, he strode toward her and dropped to one knee again.

"I await your bidding, my mistress."

Again Chloe looked uncertain. "Very well. Lie on the bed. On your back."

No longer trying to suppress his grin, Alex obeyed. He even put his hands over his head when she ordered him to. She knelt on the bed next to him, there was a second snap, and he realized that now both his wrists were fixed to the bed frame.

He jerked his arms, testing the strength of the bonds and they held firm. Some of his confidence drained away. She really did have him bound tight.

"Hey, Chloe, fun's fun, but..."

"Silence, slave." Funny thing, this time she sounded more convincing. She slapped her little whip against his chest.

The tiny strands of leather stung and he yelped. "Hey, that hurt!"

Instantly she looked contrite. "Oh, I'm sorry..." Then she dragged herself back into character. "You are my prisoner, Alex. You have to do what I say."

"Yeah, okay. But when do we get to the good part?"

"Soon, soon. First we have to establish a safe word. That's a code word so that if things get too much for you, all you have to do is say it and I'll let you free."

"Okay, sure. What's the safe word?"

She seemed to think about it for a moment. "I think the word should be...*love*."

Alex caught his breath. "*What?*"

Chloe waved her little whip under his face, letting the leather tassels caress his chin. "The code word is 'love'. All right? Say the word, and I'll set you free."

Setting his jaw, Alex settled his head back onto the pillow. No way she was going to get him to say *that* word. He'd vowed never ever to tell another woman that he loved her, not after what Mel had done to him. He didn't even use the word much.

"Okay, *Mistress*...do your worse."

* * * * *

This wasn't going well at all. Playing with her mini-whip, Chloe considered the situation carefully. Obviously Alex was upset with her and for more than just the handcuffs on his wrists. He'd been fine with being secured to the bed until she'd told him the "safe" word.

Now he glared at her, and even his previously rigid cock seemed to have lost interest in the proceedings, wilting onto his belly. Obviously the word love just wasn't safe for him. Odd. She'd often heard it used in an informal way, as in "I love your cooking," or "I'd love to do him." It didn't have to mean the deeper emotion, the romantic love between a man and woman.

As she thought about it, she'd never heard Alex use the word casually. Maybe he couldn't use it. If so, perhaps she should find out why. He didn't normally answer her questions about himself, but she wasn't normally in as persuasive a position as she was right now. Nina had spent the better part of an hour showing her how to use the mini-whip as a means of getting a man's attention. Maybe with that attention she could get some answers.

She ran the short straps of her whip along his chest, circling the nipples. Each immediately sprang to attention under the soft leather caress. Alex seemed to bite his lower lip as if trying to avoid reacting.

"You don't like the word I picked?" Chloe asked the question as casually as she could.

"Word?" Alex blinked at her as if trying to remember what she was talking about. Then his eyes narrowed in anger. "Oh, yeah, the safe word. No, I don't like it," he gritted out between clenched teeth.

She traced the muscles of his stomach. "I don't understand, Alex. It's just a word."

"Not to me it isn't. Pick another one."

Sighing, she let the whip run along the end of his penis. Obviously remembering how the tiny straps could sting, Alex lifted his head and watched her, concern in his face.

She lifted the whip off him and brandished it in his face. "Do you really think I'd hit you there? Don't you trust me at all, Alex?"

He frowned. "If I didn't trust you, I wouldn't have let you tie me up." He nodded at the rod in her hand. "I'm just not sure I trust you with something like that. You could slip with it…or something."

Chloe reached under the bed for the shoebox she'd used to store the items Nina had left with her, and pulled out the feather tickler. She held up both whip and tickler where Alex could see them. "If I switch to this, would you be happier?"

Alex examined both items and must have decided the feathers looked safer. "Okay, sure."

She ran the short, feathered rod against the tip of his cock and he groaned in appreciation, his hips writhing on the bed.

A funny little twisted grin appeared on his face. "Yeah, babe. I'm much happier."

She giggled. Nina had told her that a dominatrix didn't giggle while disciplining her slave — it spoiled the impression of control she had. She'd explained this when Chloe hadn't been able to stop laughing after first seeing her reflection wearing the outfit she now wore.

Laughter had always come easily to Chloe. She'd been the most carefree of the nymphs, with a smile and lighthearted chatter for everyone. But then she'd fallen afoul of Hera, losing her voice, and after that she'd lost her heart in her misguided love for Narcissus. She'd loved him, lost him, and finally lost her love for life. Once that last was gone, she'd had no reason to remain among the living.

Through Alex, she'd regained her life and a reason to keep it. Being with him had returned her joy. Seeing his smile, she couldn't avoid giggling now, no matter how undignified it was.

Still, dignity was part of what this game was about. Chloe regained control of her mirth and ran the tickler under Alex's nose. "I'm glad my slave has found something to laugh about."

Alex wrinkled his nose and sneezed. "Keep that thing away from my face, Chloe. I'm allergic to feathers."

This time he frowned when she giggled. "Don't think you can get me to sneeze the safe word. I won't."

That sobered her up. Alex really did have a problem with that word. She'd never get him to say it this way, and he'd only get angrier at her if she tried. Of everything she wanted, having Alex angry with her wasn't one of them.

"Perhaps I should pick another word, then. I'd hate to think of you expiring from an allergy just because you couldn't tell me to stop." She thought for a moment then grinned. Leaning over him, Chloe let her nipples rub against his chest and heard his low growl in response. It did a lot for her, too, her nipples tingling at the contact.

"Okay, Alex. Just for you, my helpless slave. The safe word is now…*artichoke*."

That returned his grin. Impishly he narrowed his eyes, and this time his voice held only playfulness. "Very well, mistress. Do your worst. You won't hear artichoke from me."

Chapter Eleven

Chloe's worst was very, very good indeed! Alex leaned his head back into the pillow, enjoying the torture his little mistress was giving him. She ran the feathered toy along his nipples, following the action with her finger, licking it first then stroking the sensitized skin. So good. He felt he could come just from her wet finger.

She pinched one of his nipples, and his head jerked up at the tiny pain. "I don't want you falling asleep on me."

Fall asleep? Alex glanced down at his cock, near throbbing in unrelieved sexual need. Every stroke she gave him made him harder. He watched a droplet of pre-cum drop to his belly, joining others to form a small puddle.

"No chance of that, babe." Alex nodded at his cock. "That looks hungry for attention, don't you think?"

Chloe dipped a finger into the puddle and stuck it into her mouth, sucking her finger with obvious relish. "Hmm, tastes terrific."

"Tastes even better from the source."

She giggled again and he nearly groaned aloud. Did Chloe know how sexy that giggle of hers was? He'd never met a woman who laughed so much during sex. All the sexy outfits, lace panties, and toys together didn't get him half as hot as her giggle did.

Eyes twinkling, Chloe lifted his cock, closing her hand around the shaft just below his glans. She leaned forward to lick the small opening in the tip. "Mmm. I think you're right, it does taste better here."

Her playfulness was going to kill him...and what a way to go. If he could get free, he'd grab those impudent shoulders of hers and roll her under him, then thrust into her at once. When she'd leaned over he'd seen how that cute little outfit of hers had no crotch. Even more, he'd seen how trimmed up her pussy hair was. Every slick fold of hers had been revealed, her glistening clit bright pink against the shortened strands.

She was wet and ready, and with his hands bound he couldn't touch her. That was the real torture tonight.

Chloe straddled his chest facing his crotch, and went to work on his cock, sucking it into her warm wet mouth. Alex nearly lost his mind at the sudden intensity. She was so good at that. For a moment he wondered if he should come in her mouth. That would end the fun tonight, and teach her a lesson in pushing a man too far.

But that hardly seemed the right thing to do. He could control it. Besides, she thought she was in control because she'd bound his hands. Let's see how much he could do without them. Maybe he could get her to release him without using any safe word.

Alex opened his eyes and realized her wide-open crotch was just below his chin, all those slick folds dripping with arousal, just inches from his face. What a fabulous view. If he lifted his head and reached out his tongue he could just touch it.

He tried it and caught her clit with the tip of his tongue. She tasted like warm aroused woman, vanilla with nutmeg, Chloe flavor. His action had taken her by surprise and she cried out, the sound muffled by his cock in her mouth.

She moved back, just a little closer to him...obviously an invitation to repeat his action. He gave her another lick, this time delving deeper into her folds before pulling back. Chloe jerked in response and practically shoved her pussy into his face.

Alex drew his head back. "Did you want something, mistress? Would you like me to eat your pussy?"

Still holding his cock in her mouth, Chloe mumbled something unintelligible.

It was all he could do not to laugh. "What was that? I can't understand you."

She sucked in his tip, long and hard, and Alex's laugh choked off in his throat. Freeing her mouth of his cock, she glanced back at him, her glare humorous. "I said, yes, I do. I want you to make me come, slave."

Alex nodded his head in mock obedience. "Yes, mistress. Right away."

He barely had to lift his head. Her pussy came right to him, and he set to work on her, licking, laving, sucking...anything he could think of to bring her to orgasm. With her sucking his penis, thinking became something of a struggle, but he worked through it. Her taste urged him on, as well as the rising tension in her thighs straddling him. He could sense her orgasm long before it hit her, both in that and because she pulled his cock out of her mouth, gasping for breath.

His mouth flooded with her essence as she came, sweet and musky. He lapped her with his tongue, reveling in her rare flavor. So responsive, his Chloe was. He'd never had a woman like her, not in taste or enthusiasm, certainly not in bed. She sprawled on top of him, still shuddering from her climax, hands grasping his shaft as if it was a lifeline.

She looked over her shoulder, her eyes still wide with excitement. Excitement and…something else. Had he ever seen that kind of warmth in a woman's eyes before?

He'd almost call it love…not that he would since that wasn't a word he used, ever. He'd sworn never to love another woman, but it possible a woman might come to love him?

That wasn't something he could control, at least not in any way that wouldn't make him a complete heel. He couldn't be mean to Chloe just to keep her from loving him.

Not when she smiled at him like that.

Chloe turned to face him, running her hands from his waist to the sides of his chest, then up onto his up stretched arms. She stared into his face, resting her hands on his biceps. "That was very nice, slave. Very nice, indeed." She nibbled on his chin, her nipples brushing his chest. "You've been very obedient. Should I reward you?"

She fingered his lips. "I'll give you one thing. My pussy, or your freedom. Pick freedom and I'll release you, but we won't make love. Pick the other and you'll get free, but not until after you come."

Was she serious? Could she really mean she wouldn't have sex with him, and she'd leave him with a case of blue-balls if he asked to be released now? Alex studied her determined face and decided that she probably did. That did it for him. His arms strained to be freed, but his cock and balls hurt worse.

"Give me your pussy, mistress."

There were no giggles in her now. "As you wish."

She positioned herself over his cock and lifted it to point to her core. Slowly she lowered herself, so slowly that Alex found himself clutching his hands into fists at the sweet torture of it. He tried raising his hips to speed the process up and she immediately put her hands on his belly, pushing him back down.

"Now, now, don't be greedy."

He said nothing but secretly Alex vowed that someday soon, he'd have her in handcuffs and would take her every which way he could in retaliation. Sweet revenge would be his.

All plans for future payback fled his head when she sank down on him in one quick drop. Encased in all that warm, moist tightness, Alex forgave her everything right on the spot. She could do anything, so long as he had her pussy around him.

She rose and sat, pumping on top of him, and Alex kept pace as best he could with his hips. His arms strained to be free, to grab her and slow her down, to speed her up, to do something…she was in control, completely in control of this sex. With no choice in the matter, Alex let her find her rhythm and keep it. Sweet ecstasy filled him as she rode him. For the first time he was letting a woman manage their sex and after a few moments, he found out something new. He found out he rather liked it.

When he came it was sudden and sharp, followed by long spasms as he flooded her pussy with his cum. He orgasmed with the intensity of lightning and thunder. Chloe came just after him, her peal of joy triumphant as her pussy milked his body dry. She collapsed on top of him, breathing heavily, her hands clutching at his shoulders.

As he recovered he heard her speaking. Soft sounds came from her lips, meaningless noise, but he thought they were words. Old words from a language he didn't know.

"What are you saying, babe?" he asked.

She turned to him, eyes wide, her hand on her mouth. Heat blazed from her cheeks. "Nothing, Alex." She licked her lips. "Nothing at all."

Alex doubted he wanted to know what it was after all. Instead he nodded to his arms. "Can I get free now?"

Chloe pulled on a string tied to the lamp near the bed and a tiny key appeared. Moments later Alex was sitting up, massaging his wrists. The skin felt tender but not bruised or torn, thanks to the heavy padding inside the cuffs.

She seemed distant as she cleaned up the room, changing from the little bondage outfit into a nightgown. Alex showered and put on his uniform in preparation for going to work.

He didn't want to go to work tonight. Not that he usually wanted to go but right now it seemed particularly wrong to leave. Something had upset Chloe and he wasn't sure what. Sex tonight had been great, better than great, if a little out of the ordinary. Alex had never been a big fan of games, but he could see how they could be useful. It had been his first time losing control that way. He smiled at how his seeming helplessness had contributed to that.

Before leaving he captured Chloe in his arms and held her tight, even when she struggled, letting her feel his strength. When she realized he wasn't going to let her go, she quit fighting him and leaned into him instead.

"Hey, babe. That was fantastic. A real mind-blower."

Eyes wide, she gazed into his face. "You liked it?"

He kissed her, a long, drawn-out kiss that left her breathless. When he let her go, she staggered a little before sitting on the bed. Alex smothered a grin. He'd really knocked her for a loop this time. "Yeah, it was a blast. We'll have to try it again sometime."

Alex's eyes were drawn to the clock. Dang, he'd be late if he didn't hurry. "Look, gotta go. I'll see you the morning."

He paused on his way out the door. "Of course, next time, you get to be the slave. Fairs fair, after all."

All the way to work Alex wondered about the funny half smile she'd gotten on her face. What did it mean when a woman smiled like that?

*   *   *   *   *

After the door closed Chloe picked up the pillow and held it to her nose. It still smelled like Alex, warm aroused man. Even though she was sexually sated, his aroma gave her a warm glow that was only partially sexual.

Good thing since it was a long time until dawn when Alex would return, and she didn't really want to pull out her new vibrator.

Clutching the pillow to her chest, she lay on the bed. Fair's fair, he'd said and he was right. She'd tried to trap him and instead she'd been the one tricked into revelations. She'd said the word. Not in English, of course, but in her ancient tongue. When she'd finished her orgasm and lay on his chest, feeling that bound strength in him, the phrase had fallen out of her.

Did the words mean anything when they were tied up with passion? Maybe not, but she'd have to be more careful. She couldn't say "I love you" to Alex when he couldn't abide the word.

Chapter Twelve

Carefully Chloe peered at the recipe card, verifying the number of eggs involved. *Yep, three of them.* Beating them, she added the melted butter, then sugar, vanilla, and flour. The last ingredients to go in were the chocolate chips.

Chloe couldn't resist taking a finger-full of the mixture and putting it in her mouth. *Mmmmm.* She closed her eyes in appreciation. Was there anything better than home-made chocolate-chip cookie dough?

After sticking the cookie sheets into the oven, she sat at the spotless kitchen table with a fresh cup of coffee. Chloe took a deep whiff of air. The rich roasted-bean smell mingled with the scent of baking cookies.

She smiled. When Alex got home he'd be so pleased. There was nothing that made a house smell more like a home than baking. Maybe he'd be so pleased that he would finally tell her that he loved her.

That thought led to a wholehearted sigh. After nearly a month of living with Alex, sharing his bed, making his food, and keeping his house, he hadn't once gone beyond stating that he was "glad she was around". Even when she posed for him for the portfolio he needed to get his degree, all he ever said was how beautiful she was and how much he appreciated her help.

In bed he always called her "babe" and told how great a lay she was. Satisfying information, for certain, but not what she wanted to hear.

It wasn't love he was talking about when he said those things. It wasn't love he was professing for her and it wasn't enough to satisfy anyone, particularly not the spell of a particular goddess who personified the subject. Aphrodite had told Chloe to make Alex love her or she'd be forced back into the never-world she'd come from. She'd been given no more than two months to do the job.

After a month he still didn't love her and she was afraid that all of the chocolate-chip cookies in the world weren't going to make a difference.

The buzz of the timer caught her attention and she pulled the finished cookies from the oven. Almost before they were cool enough to eat she had one in her mouth, unable to resist the enticing smell. As the exotic flavor of chocolate melted on her tongue, Chloe closed her eyes in ecstasy.

Praise the gods...maybe chocolate-chip cookies *would* make him love her. If these delectable little goodies didn't do it, no culinary delight possibly could.

Her cooking classes had gone splendidly. The professor, a master chef named Henri was so impressed with her work that he'd offered to find her a place in one of the local restaurants as soon as the semester ended. Unfortunately that was in six weeks, long after her deadline for winning Alex's love. If she didn't succeed there, she'd never get a real job.

Sighing, Chloe leaned her hand onto her cheek.

After four weeks here with Alex she'd learned as much as possible about this time and place. As far as she could tell she was well on the way to becoming the perfect modern woman. She'd learned to work the machines that were such a part of everyone's lives. Only driving a car was still outside of her abilities, but she watched Alex's actions every chance she got. Someday she'd even get a driver's license.

As much as possible she wanted to be a woman of this time. An independent woman with the means to supporting herself, the skills to take care of a home, and the knowledge of how to satisfy a man. Every night she had Alex groaning with happiness, both at the table and in the bedroom.

She was the perfect woman for someone like Alex. So why didn't he love her?

"Wow, Chloe, those smell fantastic!" Nina's cheerful voice as she materialized in the living room broke through her revere.

A third sigh escaped Chloe's lips. Her sister had taken to "popping in" at any time, particularly when she had fresh baking done. So far she hadn't shown up when Alex was around but Chloe figured it was only a matter of time before the pair encountered each other.

Nina professed that men were good for one thing—sex—and sometimes not even that. She already professed a low opinion of Alex just from how little money he'd spent on Chloe. She hadn't dared tell her sister that she needed to earn the man's love or risk becoming a loose spirit again.

How she'd take that news wasn't a situation Chloe wanted to see anytime soon.

Settling onto the chair next to the cookies, Nina helped herself to one. She rolled her eyes as she bit into the still warm treat. "Oh, wow, these are great. Nothing like fresh baked cookies."

She eyed Chloe's outfit, one of her nicer skirts and blouses. "You're all dressed up. Hmm, fresh cookies, sexy clothes. You wouldn't be trying to coax Alex into marriage would you?"

That hit too close to home. Blushing furiously, Chloe poured a cup of coffee for her sister.

"Not marriage," she said.

Nina stared at her, chewing slowly. "Not marriage, but something else. Otherwise why would you be staying with him? I could get you a job and a place of your own."

She leaned forward. "Chloe, have you fallen for this guy?"

Had she? Chloe hadn't thought about that possibility. She'd had a number of lovers over the years, but their relationships had been fleeting things, not needing more than passion to keep her satisfied. Aphrodite's insistence on her trying to win Alex's love had forced her to stay with him long past the point she normally would have.

She'd never before made food for a man, or cleaned his clothes. Keeping a man satisfied had involved time spent in bed, not worrying about what he liked for dinner. To stay with Alex, she'd had to know Alex, really understand him. Oddly enough, this hadn't been difficult for her. In fact it had been fun. The more she'd known, the better she'd liked the man.

That wasn't falling for him — was it?

She loved him, at least a little. That was true, although she'd never let herself say the words, at least in English.

Nina had noticed her silence. "Hmm…I don't suppose he's said he's in love with you?"

"No, he hasn't."

"Sometimes guys have trouble expressing themselves." Nina slapped her forehead. "What am I saying? Guys always have trouble expressing themselves...except when they want to fuck. Then they have NO trouble."

"He has no trouble then," Chloe confirmed. She took a hard look at Nina who clearly knew much more about men in this time than she did. Perhaps she should get her sister's advice on how to get Alex to declare himself. "I need him to love me."

"Oh?" Nina's eyes narrowed in suspicion. "Why would that be?"

"To stay human...and here." Chloe explained about Aphrodite's spell and its conditions for her release from the statue. By the time she was done Nina's face was distorted with fury.

"I might have known that bitch would've given you some task like this! She forces you to be the sex toy of a human and you have to make him love you? Men like that never fall in love!"

"He's not like that..." Chloe tried to diffuse her sister's anger. "He cares for me...just doesn't love me yet."

"Sure he cares—you're better than a blowup doll for him. But he doesn't respect you and a man won't fall in love with someone he doesn't respect. It wouldn't be good for his ego."

"Oh." Chloe made the word a small sound and rested her chin on her hands. Alex's words about her being easy on their first sexual encounter returned to her. He hadn't respected her then...it wasn't likely he respected her now.

What if Nina was right and he'd never forget how little he'd had to do to talk her into sex? He'd never love her.

"What am I going to do?"

Nina crossed her arms meaningfully. "Well, one thing is that you need to find some other way of getting free. When one of these situations comes along, there is usually an alternative way to get around it."

She thought for a moment, rubbing her chin in concentration. A sly smile crossed her face. "When you've got a problem with one god, the best thing to do is find another one—preferably a god you can work with, or one who wants something from you." She stood and spun her finger around herself, fashioning a warm coat that appeared to cover her blouse and black jeans.

"Get a coat on, we need to go to the park."

Chloe pulled her coat off the rack near the door and shoved her arms down the sleeves. "Why the park? It's cold outside."

"To see a god about a spell, that's why. This god doesn't mind anything but being cooped up inside. He's an outdoorsman."

It suddenly became clear just who her sister was talking about. Chloe froze in place. "Pan? You want me to speak to him?"

Impatiently Nina grabbed her arm and pulled her to the door. "Why not Pan? He's had the hots for you for a long time and no love for Aphrodite. I bet he'd be real happy to help you."

"He's a repulsive lecher!"

"Not in the least," Nina said. "Well," she amended, "he is a lecher. And there are the legs. But he's not so bad once you get to know him."

"You get to know him then. All he's interested in is sex."

Nina laughed. "We've got that in common, but he doesn't want me, he wants you." Chloe thought her sister sounded a little bitter. "And how does that differ from what Alex wants? You were willing to sleep with him to get your freedom."

How could she argue with that? Certainly all Alex seemed to be interested in was sex with her. Never once had they had a conversation about the future—at least not a future that included her. Alex spoke of how he intended to get a job as a photographer, possibly in a big commercial studio. He'd finish his degree, get his portfolio together, and move to New York or Los Angeles...maybe San Francisco.

He'd never spoken of her moving to those far-off places with him.

Chloe sighed. If she didn't earn his love, she wouldn't be moving anywhere but back to the spirit world. Maybe she'd better talk to Pan. If her relationship with Alex fell through it would be good to have a backup plan.

Reluctantly she followed Nina through the door.

* * * * *

The air in the park was clean and crisp, the day as clear as it was cold. A pale sun hung low in the sky, casting more light than heat on this winter's day. Deciduous trees that had lost their leaves stood with mute limbs reaching high into the sky, while evergreen bushes, pines, and firs whispered softly in the breeze. Not quite cold enough for snow, but too cold for a casual walk outside.

Chloe picked up her pace to keep up with Nina, who strode fearlessly through the deserted park. Her sister never seemed to worry about dark areas, hidden assailants, or things that go bump in the night. Timidity had never been one of Nina's qualities.

Of course, being Nemesis meant that she was far scarier than anything or anyone they were likely to meet in the park. Even the god of nature wouldn't be able to cow her sister.

Probably.

Pan was certainly enough to worry Chloe. When he'd originally looked her way and made suggestive overtures to her, she'd first been afraid to say no to him, instead fleeing him without giving him an answer. Then she'd heard some disturbing stories of the games he liked to play with his occasional lovers, and she'd become afraid to say yes.

Now she was afraid to see him at all. After knowing Alex's arms, it was hard to imagine herself in anyone else's, much less someone as rampantly sexual as Pan was.

Besides, he had hairy legs—really hairy legs—and she'd found out she was allergic to wool. Even a cashmere sweater made her skin itch. After a lovemaking session with Pan, she'd probably wind up with hives all over her legs. Or backside. Or breasts.

Or her pussy...gods above, that was one place she really didn't to have itching—at least not with an itch Alex couldn't keep scratched!

Musing over her likely upcoming rash, Chloe didn't notice when Nina came to a sudden stop, and she ran into her.

"You are so clumsy sometimes," her sister scolded. "Don't you watch where you are going?"

"Most of the time," Chloe countered. "I was just thinking about something."

Nina rolled her eyes. "I can imagine what, too. That man of yours really doesn't deserve you." She shook her head. "Well, try thinking about yourself for a change. We need to get you taken care of or you'll wind up just a disembodied voice in a cave again."

"Who will wind up in a cave...and can I come live in it with her?"

The seductive male voice came from behind a waist-high hedge next to the path. When they looked, a man stood up, his lower parts covered by the still green bushes. Chloe recognized him immediately. It was Pan with his lean face and thin goatee of a beard. He'd combed his hair to cover his horns, but she'd know those intense eyes anywhere. Just being the subject of his passionate stare made a girl feel flush with desire, even if she wasn't actually attracted to him.

He glanced once at Nina, but reserved the rest his gaze for Chloe. Immediately she no longer felt cold. Liquid heat burned through her body and she had to resist the irrational urge to take her coat off.

She wasn't the only one who must have felt too warm for outer garments. Pan wore no clothing above the waist and Chloe suddenly wondered if the hair that covered his well-built chest could possibly be as soft as it looked.

Pan smiled at her, probably noting her befuddled state and recognizing the flush in her cheeks as arousal. Of course he might not care that he'd put her in a state of desire. After all, he'd been bedding befuddled women for thousands of years. What was another nymph to him?

His eyes grew more intense and she realized that she wasn't just another nymph as far as he was concerned. She was the one that got away, and that meant she was a challenge that needed to be overcome. There was a look of triumph in that smile, which meant he thought he'd already overcome her resistance to him.

He'd bed her and leave her and that would be that.

She had to be strong and force him to help her before he had his way with her body. Otherwise she would end up another notch in his sexual belt and an echo in an empty hall.

Resistance might be futile in the long run...but she couldn't let him know that now.

Chloe defied her urge to sigh. If only Alex would come through and declare his love. Then she wouldn't have any need to deal with Pan at all.

Pan leaned over the hedge, staring at her with a lascivious grin. "You look wonderful, Echo. You've put on a pound or two."

"The last time you saw me I was starving to death. I imagine I look somewhat better now," she replied tartly.

"True enough. Being with this lover of yours must agree with you then, if you're actually eating." He gave her a once over, up and down, slowly. "Yes, true love must not mean a lack of appetite, at least not where you're concerned."

Well, it was more her cooking than Alex's love that was putting weight on her, but she wasn't about to tell Pan that.

Nina spoke up, her voice cross. "Alex doesn't love her Pan. Not really. And Chloe is in trouble because of it."

Chloe nearly groaned. She didn't really want Pan to know everything that was going on, not when he could take advantage of it. Of course he'd have the advantage anyway...but no point in telling him right away!

Pan turned to Nina, speaking in his most seductive voice. "It's Chloe now, is it? All you young nymphs, wanting modern names. And what kind of trouble is *Chloe* in?"

He glanced suspiciously at Chloe's stomach. "That human hasn't gotten you with child, has he?"

"No," she said quickly. "I'm on the pill."

"Good. Responsible of you. Can't be too careful these days. So if you aren't pregnant, what trouble could you be in?"

He reached out a hand to stroke her face, his touch leaving a trail of sensual fire behind. Chloe became very aware of how long it had been since she'd felt Alex's caress. Several hours and that was far too long. "How can I be of service to such a fair one as you?"

His emphasis on the word service had her squirming. Just being in Pan's presence made her eager for a man, any man. Even a man with legs like a goat.

At least she'd heard he was hung like a donkey. *Hee-haw!*

Of course there were other ways in which he was likely to be an ass and she had to remember those ways. Pan didn't even know the meaning of the word commitment. Besides, she was with Alex now and she knew how she would feel if he made love to another woman. Really rotten.

She wouldn't go to bed—or the bushes—or anywhere else with Pan unless she absolutely had to.

Nina butted in again. "The trouble is Aphrodite, Pan. She set things up so that if Chloe doesn't make Alex love her, she's going to wind up a spirit again."

Pan shrugged. "That's a shame, Nemesis. I'd hate to see that happen to someone as vibrant and alive as our Echo here. But if you are looking to me to make this human love her, I'm the wrong god. You need Eros and his bow to help you out."

"We were thinking that maybe you could do something...not about Alex, but to keep Chloe from having to return to the spirit world."

Pan stroked his long goatee with his nimble fingers. Chloe watched, knowing how talented those hands of his were, how they would touch and finger and probe her sensitive skin...he'd be a much more sensitive lover than Alex was...

She shook her head violently. She had to stop thinking thoughts like this around Pan. It really wasn't fair to Alex to compare him to a god whose very existence was the need for sensual satisfaction. Of course Alex wasn't as talented as Pan, but he had lots of other good qualities.

If he'd only declare love for her, he'd have every quality she needed.

Pan quit stroking his beard. "There is something I could do. I could see that you got reinstated as a nymph."

Hope filled Chloe. Why, that would be wonderful, if she couldn't be with Alex. She'd be a nymph again, just like in the old days, before she'd fallen in love with Narcissus. "Could you really do that?"

He snapped his fingers. "Of course. I'm the god of the woodlands after all. I can pick who attends me and how. I could make you a nymph again easily. Not even Hera would deny me that right. It would mean serving me, of course."

"Serve you?" Chloe's heart sank, although she wasn't surprised to hear his conditions.

Pan reached out and collected one of her long locks of hair, stroking as he'd done his beard. "You wouldn't deny me what is rightfully mine, would you, Echo? All the nymphs in the forest have served me at one time, or another. Except you, my pretty one. You refused my advances, claiming a bad case of love for that silly fool, Narcissus."

She tried to move away, but he seized her arms, half pulling her into the hedge. His fierce stare froze her in place. "Now you need my help. I will help you, but I want what should have been mine to begin with. I want your promise to give me your willing body in exchange for my help."

"Willing body?"

He released her, and she nearly fell backward. "Of course. What do you think I am, a ravisher of reluctant women?" He frowned at her. "No woman, human, goddess, or nymph has ever entered my bed unwillingly, or been left unsatisfied as a result."

Gathering her shattered composure, Chloe raised her head to glare at him. "You say that, but not everyone you've bedded did so by desire."

A twisted leer crossed his face. "All right, so some women needed some persuasion, but I've never forced a woman…unlike some gods, I've never had to."

He crossed his arms and again she felt his animal magnetism. Too bad she couldn't bottle it. Essence of Pan—it was the ultimate aphrodisiac. It would sell for millions of dollars.

"When I've wanted a woman, she's been mine and it was always her desire by the time we reached that point. You will be the same as any other woman, little Echo, and you'll be happier for it."

He waved an impatient hand. "Go now and think on what I've said. If you come to me willingly I'll save you from the spirit world. You will be my love for that time, and a nymph for the always after. You will regret nothing."

Pan stepped back, giving them a full view of his body, including his very full loincloth before fading into the shadows of the trees behind him. Chloe gaped at what she'd been able to see. The god really was built like a donkey!

She turned to see a wistful smile on Nina's face. "He really is something, isn't he?"

"He must be, to impress you." Curiosity got the better of her. "How many times have you been with Pan?"

Nina shook her head as if clearing it of a bad dream. "Me? Oh, maybe once or twice." She shrugged elaborately. "He's good, no doubt about that, but if you think Alex has commitment problems, Pan is the ultimate in relationship avoidance. No one keeps his attention for long. Not that I've looked for a relationship with anyone," she quickly added.

Chloe sighed. "That's probably the only reason he wants me...because he hasn't had me yet."

Nina grimaced. "True enough. But you aren't looking for more anyway." She hugged Chloe, brimming over with excitement. "He'll make you a nymph again, Chloe. Isn't that exciting? That's an even better solution than getting Alex to love you."

Chloe smiled in return, but inside she wasn't so certain. Sure, being human had its problems but she'd learned to cope with most of them. It would be okay to run through the forests again, but part of her would always long for her kitchen and its microwave oven.

Part of her would always long for Alex's arms as well.

Truth was, she'd much rather have Alex to love — that is, have Alex's love — than be a free woodland nymph again.

Chloe linked arms with her sister and ran with her to the edge of the park, trying to ignore that lingering misthought.

Had she really told herself that she wanted to love Alex?

* * * * *

Pan watched the pair leave from his place behind the tree. When he wanted to be invisible, it just took a flick of his fingers to make himself that way. It was good to be a god. Magic was handy to have, particularly when you were a god with hooves instead of feet. Whenever he wanted to seduce a fair young thing, he'd sometimes give his legs a human look, even doing away with his horns to make himself seem normal. Having a lover who shared characteristics with a goat usually bothered human women, even if they did enjoy his other animalistic qualities. They rarely objected to the inhuman size of his cock.

Maybe that was why Echo was so resistant to his charms. He hadn't bothered to glamour his appearance for her. After all, few of the other nymphs cared. Nemesis had even complimented his fleece on one occasion when he'd entertained her, and told him that his horns made him look "hot".

When had that been? Pan had to think about it...it had been at least two, three centuries back. They'd been at an Olympian party, and both had gotten a little drunk on Bacchus' holiday punch. One thing had led to another and a wild week had been enjoyed by both of them. What a time they'd had.

But later on he'd met someone else, a vestal virgin looking for a change in her life. That had been too much of a challenge to pass up, particularly since he'd again gotten a little worse for drink. He'd intended to call Nemesis later to explain, but she'd avoided him, and then later on the opportunity hadn't come up. The next time they'd met, she'd behaved distant, barely speaking two words to him when he'd left with another willing nymph, blonde and big-breasted. He'd told himself that one body was pretty much the same as another, and tried not to care that the dark-haired nymph no longer would return his calls.

Echo and Nemesis reached the edge of the park and made the turn to leave. Pan caught one last glance of them moving through the exit, Nemesis' short-cropped dark head next to the long-haired beauty of Echo.

Maybe once he'd spent a little one-on-one time with Echo, he'd talk Nemesis into joining them for a threesome. He would pleasure Echo with his tongue while Nemesis went down on him. He imagined that dark head of hers between his thighs, taking his cock deep in her mouth, running her tongue down its length, sucking it. *Gods*, his prick ached just thinking about it. He needed some relief.

Casting a cautious glance around the area, he pulled out his engorged member and ran his hand along it. It was magnificent, thick, heavy, and long. The best cock in Olympus he'd been told more than once. He'd known thousands of pussies, debauched hundreds of virgins, and had countless encounters with the mouths and assholes of others. Through the centuries he'd enjoyed the touch of many, many women, and more than a few men, although that game had gotten old and he didn't play it much anymore. Even so, after all this time, he still liked to take things into his own hands from time to time. Leaning against the tree behind him, he closed his fist around his cock and worked it up and down with practice skill.

In his palm every ridge and vein was familiar, every stroke satisfied.

Pan closed his eyes and gave in to the sensation. *Oh yes, like that. Just a little more…*

"Aren't you a little old to be jerking off?"

Aphrodite's frigid observation hit his concentration like a bucket of ice water and his erection wilted. Furious, Pan covered himself and turned to face her, and found her standing next to his tree. Her lean form wore blue this time, a garment that revealed all her glorious curves, and with her long blonde hair she could've been very attractive if it hadn't been for the cold amusement in her face.

"Aphrodite, don't you have anything better to do than to spy on others?"

She smirked. "No, not really. I'm here to watch out for those who look to me, Pan. Like Chloe."

"You mean Echo? She's not yours, goddess. She's mine and I'll have her soon."

"She wants to be called Chloe now. You might get her name right, women like that. And you can only have her if she comes to you willingly, Pan. That was established long ago. You can't take what isn't given."

"I told her that. She knows. But she will come willingly. When she gets desperate enough."

The goddess ran a perfectly manicured finger along his arm. It left a sensual trail and he caught his breath. Her smell...lilacs and roses and a hint of sweet rosemary. Pan's nostrils flared and his cock throbbed into awareness. Almost he reached for her before remembering who she was. Sudden fear again killed his ardor.

"I'm warning you, Pan. I've plans for Chloe and her young man. You or anyone else interferes and I'll see to it that you pay a penalty for it. Remember that."

He backed away, hands up. "I'll take nothing that isn't offered freely. I know the rules. But you can't control the game completely, goddess. The players have free will, and can make their own decisions. *You* remember *that*."

"I count on their free will, little god."

Fury overcame his fear. "You don't scare me, goddess. I'm a god and there is nothing you can do to me."

"Oh, can't I?" Her silky smooth voice held some meaning and promise he didn't like. "I personify love, and that's something that even gods need. You interfere with my plans and perhaps I'll show you what I could do to you."

"You think you could deny me love?" Pan's crooked smile took over his face. "I can have any woman I want and you can't stop that."

Aphrodite waved her elegant hand. "There is a difference between sex and love, but believe what you want."

"I will." She was so certain of herself, so sure she had all the answers. Suppose he turned things around? "What about your love life, goddess of love? I haven't seen your beloved Hephaistos around lately."

It was well known that the goddess' marriage didn't appear to be the happiest in the pantheon. In fact, it was rumored that Aphrodite would have divorced the god who forged Zeus' thunderbolts if she could.

The goddess's eyes narrowed, a clear sign his barb had hit home. "You will leave my husband out of this, Pan, or I will see to it that you suffer for it."

Pan laughed and bowed mockingly. "Don't be too certain of that, mighty goddess. You don't frighten me. I'm not subject to your whims like the mortals and those of the minor ranks of Olympus are."

He whisked himself out of her sight, leaving Aphrodite furiously tapping her perfectly tied sandal on the ground.

"We will see about that, oh mighty god Pan," she told the emptiness where he'd been, then dematerializing herself leaving only her words to echo in the clear air of the park. "Watch and see, I may have the last laugh on you yet."

Chapter Thirteen

Alex looked around the deserted apartment. Where had Chloe gone? He checked the bedroom and the bathroom. No sign of her. He checked in the kitchen. No appearance of dinner underway. Unusual for her as she generally had that meal well underway by the time he got back from school. He wouldn't tell anyone this, but he'd gotten used to her having supper ready when he got home.

Frowning he examined the plate of chocolate chip cookies on the table and the partially drunk cups of coffee. It looked like Chloe had had company. He didn't mind, of course. It was fine if she had friends in. Although the only friend he knew of was her sister Nemesis, or Nina, or whatever she was called, and while he hadn't met Nina yet, he couldn't say for sure that she was a real friend. Something told him that Nina didn't exactly approve of Chloe living with him.

He helped himself to one of the cookies on the plate. *Oh man, delicious!* Where had Chloe learned to make these, they were just like his mother used to make. Good old Mom, she'd really like Chloe, a lot more than she'd ever liked Mel. Mom had always said Mel didn't really care about him, that she was after one thing, his money.

Mom had Mel pegged, all right.

He wondered what she'd say Chloe wanted. It might be interesting to find out. It had been a long time since he'd seen his mother and with the end of classes coming up... Maybe he and Chloe could take a trip out to California and visit her.

Alex looked at the clock and frowned. Where was Chloe anyway? She'd had class in the early afternoon, but she must have come home. The fresh cookies told him that.

He helped himself to two more. Couldn't spoil his dinner if dinner wasn't even underway yet. Sitting down in the living room, he turned on the television, looking for distraction. A show came on...some kind of comedy with a laugh track, smart-alecky lines, and young people, including a number of young women, none of whom looked like they weighed more than a hundred pounds each. Their skinny frames initially attracted him, but couldn't hold his interest long.

Too thin. They looked like little girls, not like his Chloe.

Alex sat back in his seat, basking in satisfaction. Chloe was a woman who looked like a woman. She'd put on some weight since living with him...all the good cooking she was doing, but it looked good on her. Made her seem—substantial. Not like a wood nymph or a dream, but like a real woman.

She'd come a long way since he'd first met her, unable to speak, read, or do much besides make love. But heaven above, could she make love. And that was one thing that hadn't changed, she was still the best lay he'd ever had. It kept getting better, too.

Sometimes he wondered how he could have gotten so lucky. He knew she'd hadn't a lot of choices after getting kicked out of her statue. He'd taken her in because he'd felt responsible, but they'd gone beyond that long ago.

She could move out, find a place of her own. The classes she'd taken had given her the ability to fend for herself. Alex had no doubt that she could find a good job in a restaurant somewhere after tasting some of her specialties during the past month. Still she stayed with him.

The sex between them was good...hell, it was great. If it got much better, he'd probably have a heart attack or need Viagra to keep up with her. Maybe both.

Alex glanced at the clock. Nearly six and she still wasn't home. Disgruntled he went to the kitchen and opened a beer, helping himself to another cookie as he passed the plate.

Alex took a big swig from the bottle. Excellent! Chloe had the best taste, always seemed to know what to get and yet how to stretch a dollar. He gave her a pittance to keep the house going, and she managed to make it go further than even his mother could have done.

Yeah, Mom would probably really like Chloe. They should go visit her.

He glanced again at the clock. It wasn't like her to be gone so long. A touch of concern filled him. Maybe something had happened to her? If she was out with that sister of hers, the sex-queen, who knows what could go wrong? Should he call the police?

And say what? Tell them that his live-in girlfriend, a former nymph and statue-come-to-life had gone missing? That was sure to make the boys-in-blue happy. Better to wait a little; she'd be home soon. If not, he'd go looking for her.

Look for her where? He didn't have any idea where she would have gone. He didn't really know how she spent her days, other than the class she was taking. He'd picked her up several times and met her teacher. An okay guy. Rather taken with Chloe, even promising to get her a job after she completed the course.

That would be something, for a woman in his house to bring in money. Mel never would have done it, but then Chloe was nothing like Mel and he very much liked her differences.

Chloe was so quiet, somewhat shy, even a little innocent in ways. She probably didn't even realize how many of the guys in her class were interested in her. Well, the straight guys at least. He'd shown a little muscle when a one of her classmates had gotten too friendly and put his arm around her. He'd grabbed the guy's arm and twisted it. Not hard, just enough to get the guy to back off.

Alex took another swig out of his bottle. It was a good thing he'd been there. Chloe needed him around to keep riffraff like that away. That joker was just like the guys on this sitcom. They took a girl and used her for sex, got her to take care of their apartment, and then didn't giving her the respect she was due. *They'd never tell her how much she meant to them...*

Abruptly he sat up and turned off the set. It was a little too close to his situation with Chloe. For some time now he'd felt a twinge of guilt every time he'd come home to find her cleaning the apartment or fixing his dinner. He'd let her move in because she'd no place else to go and he'd felt sorry for his part in putting her into that situation. It was her idea to keep their relationship sexual...not that he was complaining. But now she'd taken over the place on her own. It was nice but he didn't know if he really wanted her doing it.

It almost felt like they were married. Here he was, actually thinking of taking her home to meet his mother.

He'd better keep a tighter grip on things or he really would find himself saddled with her for good.

And how bad would that be?

Well, it wasn't that it would be bad. But he just wasn't sure if he was ready for that yet. Sure, Chloe was a great babe and all, but he didn't really know that much about her. He didn't even know if she really liked him.

She hadn't said anything about it. Never told him how she felt about him.

And what would you do if she did?

Alex ignored the little voice that kept speaking up, the voice of his conscience. Chloe hadn't told him she loved him, so he had no business saying it to her. Even if he did love her. Which he didn't.

At least he thought he didn't.

But he sure wished that she would come home.

Alex helped himself to a fifth and sixth cookie and ate them quickly, barely noting how good they were. He washed them down with the last of his beer.

Only one cookie remained on the plate. He'd had so many already and she'd probably intended them for dessert. She'd be disappointed if he ate them all.

On the other hand, what could she do with one cookie? She'd already had some earlier. Alex picked it up and ate it slowly, savoring its chocolate and vanilla goodness. He closed his eyes in appreciation.

Just like Mom used to make — Chloe sure knew how to cook!

* * * * *

Alex picked at the food on his plate, his appetite for it gone. It was tasty enough but he couldn't find the enthusiasm he normally had for his meals. Probably ate too many cookies, he reasoned.

Or maybe it was something else. Chloe had been so quiet when she'd returned from her walk in the park. He'd tried to ask why she'd gone there in the first place. The park was no place for a woman alone during the cold winter months, but she'd only said she wasn't alone, that her sister had been with her. But she'd been so cold when she'd gotten back, and not just from the weather.

She'd barely spoken to him since coming home, not even to scold him for eating all the cookies. She acted as if she hadn't cared at all.

Oddly enough, that hurt. He'd expected some sort of reaction from her, if only for him spoiling his dinner. Instead she'd simply put the plate in the dishwasher and started preparing the food. Oven-fried chicken, one of his favorite meals. Normally he'd eat three pieces.

Only one on his plate had been finished and he toyed with part of a second. Chloe didn't seem to have much appetite either, she'd finished one leg and most of her vegetables, but it was more like she was going through the motions than enjoying a meal.

Neither of them had said a word.

Finally Alex couldn't take the silence any longer. He threw his napkin onto the table—another thing she'd introduced into the apartment, along with new silverware and plates not made of plastic—and growled.

"I'm sorry I ate all the damn cookies. They were so good I couldn't help myself."

Chloe looked up at him, her face startled as if she'd forgotten he was even there. Her brow wrinkled as if she couldn't understand what he was talking about.

She shrugged her shoulders. "The cookies? They were made to be eaten."

"Yeah, but not all at once." He frowned. "Isn't that why you're mad at me?"

A funny look stole across her face as if the whole idea of her being angry with him was so farfetched that she'd never even considered it possible. She shook her head. "I'm not angry with you, Alex."

"Oh, you could have fooled me. You've barely spoken to me this evening. You act like I've done something wrong."

Again she shrugged. "You've done nothing. You are what you are. There is nothing to be angry about."

This was worse than her yelling at him. Come to think of it, Chloe had never raised her voice to him, outside of that one time when he'd called her easy. Maybe she didn't care anything about him, not even enough to get mad at him.

"Doesn't anything I do bother you?"

She hesitated, as if she were going to say something then shook her head as if she'd changed her mind.

She gave him a small smile, but he could see the sadness in her eyes. "You are what you are, Alex."

What did that mean? That she didn't expect better of him than to not eat a bunch of cookies before dinner, or that she didn't expect anything from him at all.

Alex cleared his throat. "I was thinking about something before you got home. My Mom lives in L.A.

and it's been a while since I've seen her. Maybe we can go to visit her when school is over."

Chloe's eyes lit up. "You want us both to go?"

"Yeah, she'd get a kick out of you. Of course we wouldn't tell her about you coming from a statue or being an ancient Greek nymph. She might not understand all that."

For the first time since coming home, she smiled and her excitement gave him a thrill he hadn't expected.

"When would we go?"

"My last class will be in May. We could go in early June."

Some of her excitement dimmed. "That's four months from now."

"Yeah. Not that long. You'll have finished your class, and if you have a job offer you can simply wait until after the trip to start."

"No." She shook her head. "Too long."

The sadness was back in her eyes and as she turned away from him something told Alex that there was a lot more than time at stake here.

He seized her arms. "What do you mean, too long, Chloe? Why is four months too long to wait for a trip?"

She looked up at him, her eyes filling with tears. "I might not be able to stay that long, Alex. I might…have to go away."

She was going to leave him? The uneasy feeling he'd had all day developed into the ache of impending loss. Releasing her, he stepped back, struggling to control his anger at this unexpected pain. "Why, Chloe, why would you leave? You don't want to be with me?"

"I do...but I might not be able to."

Suspicion rose in him. "Does your sister have anything to do with this?"

She startled and he thought he detected a little bit of guilt in her expression. He'd bet anything that sex-driven nymph was involved.

Chloe shook her head. "No. Not really. Nina wants to help me."

"She's helping? If you need help, why can't I help you?"

"It isn't that easy, Alex."

"Why not? Why don't you tell me what the problem is?"

"I can't. The goddess said... I can't that's all."

"The goddess?" Alex frowned. "Aphrodite said you couldn't tell me something?"

Chloe grabbed their plates and rose to her feet. "Don't push it, Alex. Goddesses can be very bad people to make angry. I learned that lesson the hard way a long time ago. I can't tell you what the problem is."

He subsided, fuming a little. "Just like Melody, running off when things get a little rough."

Chloe gaze swung over to him. "Who's Melody?"

He might as well tell her. "My ex-girlfriend. When I decided to leave my job and become a photographer, she dumped me."

"Did you love her, Alex?"

Chloe's voice was quiet, but he could hear the intensity in it. Should he confess all to her? Maybe she'd understand better if he did.

"Yeah, I loved her and she just about tore my heart out when she left."

"I see." Chloe's face looked thoughtful. "I suppose she told you she loved you."

"Every day, every hour, right up to the moment when she packed her bags." Alex grimaced. "I can't stand the word now, Chloe. It means nothing if there isn't real feeling behind it."

"No. It doesn't." She sighed and turned the water on to rinse the dishes. "I promise, Alex, I won't run off unless there is no other choice. And if I can, I will tell you why I had to leave."

* * * * *

Their lovemaking that night didn't satisfy either of them, and Alex left for work almost as soon as it was over. For the first time Chloe pulled out the vibrator Nina had given her and used it to bring herself to a climax.

Even so, it wasn't really enough.

Pan wanted her and would help her by reinstating her as a nymph. Not the solution she wanted, but it would keep her from becoming a spirit again.

Her only other option was to hope that Alex would declare love for her. At least she knew now why he didn't want to do it.

The goddess had told her she needed his love to stay human. She was beginning to think she needed it for an even bigger reason, too.

Without Alex's love she didn't want to even keep living.

Chapter Fourteen

Nina watched Chloe poke a careful finger into her dough, checking to see if it had risen enough to knead. Her sister had explained that she was making a new recipe that required two risings, this being the first.

Baking fresh bread when it could be purchased at a store for nearly the same price. Chloe said she did it because Alex liked fresh baked bread better than store bought.

Nina shook her head. Too much trouble to go to just to please a man, but then Chloe always seemed to go to a lot of trouble to please her human. She'd seen the man once from a distance, and didn't see the attraction, but obviously Chloe did. She did many things for her human, including putting off Pan and refusing to give him a firm answer. The god wasn't the most patient of immortals.

After a sip from her cup of coffee, she approached the subject again. "I don't understand you. You could go to Pan tonight and be a nymph again by tomorrow. You'd be safe from any harm Aphrodite might try and dish out... Pan protects his own. Gods above, if you really wanted to stay with this man, you could even do that. Just go to Pan after your human goes to work this evening. You could return to him later."

Chloe spoke finally. "As a nymph I'd return."

Nina shrugged. "It wasn't like he'd notice the difference."

"He would, eventually. Besides, I think he'd know something had happened. I doubt a woman who's been with Pan wouldn't show some signs. He isn't a gentle lover...or so I've heard."

She noticed Chloe flinch. "Pan's not gentle, but he isn't abusive. He'd never really hurt you, at least not physically." Chloe gave her a quick glance and she added hastily. "You aren't afraid of him are you?"

"Not afraid...exactly. Alex can be aggressive sometimes, but I know he wouldn't hurt me."

"Pan won't hurt you either. Just give you the best bedding of your existence."

Chloe giggled nervously. "If he's that good, why don't you bed him, Nina? I bet you could keep up with him far better than I could. Obviously you're interested."

Nina shook her head. "I'm not interested in fucking Pan. I've been with him before, and he with me, and that was that. We don't want each other anymore."

Another giggle escaped her sister. "Oh, really? I'm not so certain of that. I believe you have a bit of a thing for him. Maybe you like guys with really hairy legs?"

"There is nothing wrong with Pan's legs! The fleece is soft and warm and the hooves give him traction. That can be a good thing," Nina said slyly.

"I'm sure, but I'm very fond of Alex's legs as they are, he has all the traction he needs, and I love his toes."

"Love his toes, huh? Love anything else?"

Chloe faltered. Her gaze dropped to the dough in front of her and she didn't look at Nina. Pulling the lump toward her, she pounded it with her fist and proceeded to knead it with a regular stroke, born of long practice.

A strange idea rolled into Nina's head and her heart sank into her stomach. She raised an unsteady hand to point at Chloe.

"You've fallen in love with him, haven't you?" she accused.

Chloe kneading stopped for an instant then resumed. She didn't answer Nina or meet her gaze.

"You have! That's why you won't go to Pan. You're still hoping that dolt will admit to loving you."

"No, I'm not expecting that." Chloe's voice was sad, resigned. "Alex can't love anyone, not anymore. He had a bad relationship…"

"Everyone has a bad relationship from time to time. It makes you wary of loving the wrong person, but he couldn't find anyone less wrong than you. Doesn't he know how wonderful you are?"

Chloe shaped the dough into a narrow rod and covered it with a damp cloth. "I think he knows. I think he really cares for me. But I don't think he's willing to admit anything of the sort. He won't use the word love because he sees that as a commitment and he can't commit to anyone."

She sat on the stool near the counter and stared at her cup. Nina stroked her sister's arm. "Oh, you poor kid. You really have it bad."

Chloe sipped her coffee and smiled wryly. "I'm going to miss coffee. There are a lot of things I'll miss."

"Not necessarily. You can still go to Pan…" Nina's voice trailed off as she watched Chloe shake her head. A tear eased from one of Chloe's eyes and trickled down her cheek, only to get dashed away.

"I can't, Nina. I've thought about it and I just can't have sex with Pan, even if it would save me. It would be a betrayal of Alex, of how I feel about him."

Another tear joined the first and fell unheeded to the countertop. Chloe rested her chin on her hand and stared into space. "Nina, I can't help it. I'm in love with him and I'm committed to him, even if he isn't to me."

Nina watched her sister's quiet tears, hearing the despair in her voice. She treated sex as a game, one she held the winning position in. She kept control—of the situation, of her partners, and most importantly, of herself. It kept her safe, but it made her empty, too. Having Chloe to talk to, to laugh with...she'd grown to love it if only because with Chloe she could be herself. She never could do that with her sex partners.

How long had it been since she'd felt even a portion of what Chloe felt for her human? Maybe never. Well, that wasn't exactly true. She'd been briefly infatuated with someone once and had her heart trampled as a result. Not that she'd ever admit it to anyone, particularly a certain male deity with horns and really hairy legs. No, not that oversexed, majestic prick. Back when she'd been a young impressionable nymph, Pan had been the man who'd showed her how sex should be, all wild passion—and no promises. He'd dumped her a mere week after the initiation of their love affair, chasing after a vestal virgin instead. No, it hadn't been a love affair, better she called it a sex affair.

A rampant, over-the-top, screw in every room, forest, and field sex affair. She'd been exhausted when he'd left, sore in every orifice, but brokenhearted all the same. She wondered if he could still make her sore...she was a lot tougher than she used to be.

Funny how she'd pretty much forgotten all that. It wasn't until she'd seen him again that she'd remembered how good it had been, and how bad. Then he'd barely even looked at her, lusting after poor little Chloe instead. Chloe who didn't even want him, which was probably one of the reasons he wanted her.

Typical male behavior, only wanting what he couldn't have. Would he listen to Chloe if she told him she was in love with someone else? No. He'd be selfish, not caring about what she wished for so long as he got what he wanted. All males were like that.

Well, she admitted to herself, Nick wasn't like that. When he'd fallen in love with Violet, it was her wishes he'd heeded. Nina had tried to seduce him but he'd refused her, and chose to return to stone even though screwing her would have given him the freedom he craved. He hadn't wanted to hurt Violet.

If only Chloe's man would do that and fall in love with her. Even after two months of being with her, the human was still completely self-absorbed, only seeing his own wants, not anyone else's. That dolt was just like Nick when he'd had the name Narcissus. Just a big, dumb clod staring into a pond, mesmerized by his own reflection after being hit with Eros' arrow and falling in love with himself...*wait a minute*!

Nina sat up, a wriggle of excitement filling her. *Eros' arrow!* Maybe that was the answer. If she remembered correctly, Eros and his wife, Psyche, were taking a brief cruise in the Caribbean, on The Love Boat, or something like that. She'd overheard him at one of the Olympian nightclubs, complaining about how he couldn't take more than a very small bow with him due to packing regulations. All of his other weaponry would be at their home on Mount Olympus.

Surely Eros wouldn't mind if she borrowed one. He'd probably be delighted to see love blossom for Chloe. After all, that's what he did — make love blossom, one arrow at a time. Of course she'd have to hide what she planned from Chloe. Her sister wouldn't like her human male being forced to love her. She'd probably get all worried about his free will or something.

Nina reached over to squeeze Chloe's hand. "Honey, don't cry. I've got a feeling things will work out."

Chloe used a napkin to blot her reddened eyes. A brave smile curved her lips. "I wish I could be as certain as you."

They hugged, and Nina stepped back, prepared to leave. "I've got to run, Chloe. There's an errand I need to do, but I'll try and be back later. I'd like to meet this human of yours."

"Alex, Nina. His name is Alex."

Nina laughed. "Okay, just for you, Chloe. I'd like to meet Alex."

She snapped her fingers, and used her magic to transport her to Mount Olympus.

* * * * *

Nina stared around the god's mansion in open admiration. So this was how the upper pantheon lived. Not bad, not bad at all!

Psyche was an excellent decorator. Her color choices showed a lot of soul. Magenta and peach colors in the bedroom, blues and greens in the living room, but all nicely tied together with a sand-colored marble floor and palest blue sky color for the ceiling. It was elegant, but not cool. Warm, inviting, instantly relaxing, a perfect environment for sex.

She thought about her little apartment in the low-rent district of the Elysian Fields. The red and black color scheme she'd used seemed far too harsh compared to this subtle approach. Maybe once this was over she could have a chat with Psyche and get some ideas for improving her personal space.

Provided the god's wife was speaking to her. "Borrowing" someone else's equipment without permission was frowned upon in Olympian circles, but it was an emergency. She couldn't wait for the god and his wife to get back from vacation, not with her sister's life at stake.

Eros wouldn't mind, and he might not even notice. She'd return the bow as soon as possible, and the arrow…he had to have enough of those to not realize he was missing one arrow.

Carefully she hunted about for the armory. It was probably off the peach and magenta bedroom. She took a moment to admire the bed, chuckling when she stroked the ultra-smooth fabric of the peach comforter and the surface rippled under her hand.

A waterbed? Eros and Psyche slept on a waterbed? How seventies!

One of the bedposts caught her eye, and she smiled at the subtly placed restraint hook. *Why Eros, you naughty boy! Does your mother know you practice bondage?*

She opened a door and discovered a walk-in closet. *Oh my.* Nina blinked in astonishment at the array of sex toys, whips, ticklers, restraints, and dildos arranged neatly on shelves or hanging on the pegboard that lined the walls. In one corner were two five-gallon dispensers, one of fragrant massage oil, the other some sort of super-lube.

My, my, my. Now she understood why the pair always had that look of sated bliss on their faces. Her collection seemed pathetic compared to this.

She was learning a lot about the celestial pair, but that wasn't her purpose. This wasn't lifestyles of the divinely decadent, and she wasn't on a tour. She needed to find where Eros kept his spare bows. Another door seemed to beckon. Hoping it wasn't the bathroom, which would surely prove a distraction, Nina tried it.

Bingo! She found a room with racks of archery equipment. Well over two dozen gold, wood, and silver bows hung on the racks, both strung and unstrung. Next to each was a quiver of arrows. Nervously, Nina picked her way through the bristling display. She'd been much more at home in the walk-in closet than here. While she'd taken basic archery from Artemis as a young nymph—it was a required course—she'd never really enjoyed it. Sex she understood, weaponry she didn't.

Some of the bows were huge, at least as tall as she was. Too big. There wasn't any way she'd be able to draw one of these monsters, much less hide them. Her task required stealth. She knew that Eros had taken a small bow with him. Surely with this many in his collection, there would be one or two others small enough for her to carry concealed and that she'd have the strength to draw.

She searched the room. *There, over in the corner.* A small short bow, only about two feet long. It hardly looked like it belonged with the others it was so little. It wasn't even made of gold but some sort of reddish wood. Next to it was a quiver of arrows, also shorter than usual. Nina pulled one of the arrows to examine it. The arrowhead was made of some kind of gold metal. She admired the workmanship on the head. It was beautiful, but looked wickedly sharp. She shuddered, glad it wasn't her body that would be hit with that point.

Nina flicked her fingers and a cloak appeared in her hands. Carefully she wrapped both the arrow and bow in it, to conceal them from her fellow Olympians' eyes. While she could do small magic like making a cloak out of thin air, she'd need to walk back to her home before doing anything as major as transporting. Magic tended to attract too much attention.

She examined the cloak-wrapped bundle. The shape of the bow was somewhat hidden. This would work for now but she'd have to find something else to hide the bow before taking it back to Earth. Maybe she had something in her apartment that would work.

Finished, she returned to the living room, making sure she'd left no sign of her passage through the rooms. If Eros really wanted to, he'd be able to figure out pretty quickly who'd been here, but it would be another several days before he and Psyche would be home. She'd be able to return the bow long before then.

She might even take a vacation herself just in case he did figure out she'd taken it. Someplace warm, like Tahiti. Nina could imagine herself sunning on a beach in a colorful pareo, or swimming in warm turquoise-colored water, acquiring a tan while the heat died down. Sounded like paradise.

She could stand a little paradise for a while. It wouldn't be long before Eros forgot about her transgression. No more than twenty or thirty years, max.

Sighing, Nina prepared to leave. It didn't matter if she did get caught, or punished. Someone had to save Chloe. If her sister went back to the spirit world, that would be far worse punishment than anything they could do.

One way or another, Alex was going to fall in love with Chloe. If the dolt wouldn't do it on his own, she'd provide a little pointed help to do the job.

Clutching the cloak wrapped bundle to her chest, Nina slipped through the unlocked back door and headed for her home.

Chapter Fifteen

Chloe looked at the clock. Just past four o'clock. She had a couple of hours before Alex got home, just enough time to finish baking bread for dinner. Smiling sadly, she got up to check the dough under its damp cloth. Not quite finished rising yet, she'd check it again in a few minutes.

With Nina gone, she was at a loss for something to do. The apartment was clean, the laundry all done. She's prepared dinner, a nice casserole and salad, which were waiting in the refrigerator. All she needed to do was put the casserole in the oven with the bread.

She didn't really want to watch television. Lately the shows had all seemed tedious. Two people would fall in love then fight continuously until the end of the program when they'd miraculously make up. Why did they always go through that period of fighting? Didn't they realize how lucky they were to have someone who loved them?

Didn't they realize how lucky they were to have a future?

If she were a character on one of these shows, she would know how lucky she was. She didn't have a future or someone who loved her.

Aphrodite had warned her that she needed to get Alex's love within two months or the spell that had turned her human would fail. She'd return to the spirit world, barely able to make herself solid and if she weren't close to her statue when the spell failed, she might drift away, unable to anchor herself to this world at all.

At least at the museum she'd be able to see Alex occasionally.

As of yesterday, her two months were up and he hadn't expressed love for her at all. Anytime now she expected to hear the goddess's voice, telling her she needed to return to the museum.

Her gaze fell on the small bookcase she'd added to the living room, a castoff she'd found on the street on garbage day. It had only taken a little work to repair the broken support for one of the shelves. Now it stood filled with paperback novels, of romance and adventure, places she'd never been, places she'd never see. She'd become an avid reader in the past two months, making up for thousands of years without stories.

Yet another thing she would miss, reading a good novel. Chloe considered reading one now, but none of the old ones appealed to her, and the new ones were all too long to finish quickly. She'd hate to leave and not know how the story ended.

She hated to leave anyway, but that was how her story was going to end.

Would Alex miss her? She supposed so. He'd certainly miss having clean clothes, home-cooked meals, and a tidy apartment. Maybe he'd get a clue once she was gone and realize that commitment wasn't such a bad thing, and that the least a woman deserved was to be loved.

All people need love, humans, gods, and wood nymphs—even Alex needed love. He just didn't realize it yet.

A large book on top of the bookcase caught her attention. She picked it up and discovered it was photo album. In the inside cover was Alex's full name and the class he was taking.

Alex's portfolio! She'd wondered how he'd been doing on that. Since he used the lab at the university to develop his pictures, she'd seen very few of them, and he'd been reluctant to bring anything home to show her.

He must have brought it in yesterday while she was working on dinner. Maybe he'd intended to show it to her last night, but feeling how short time was for her, she'd been too eager to get to bed with Alex. They'd skipped their usual after-dinner talk in the living room.

Sitting on the couch, Chloe opened the book to leaf through it. There were pictures of her, beautiful images. Some were black and white, some color. All were perfectly composed, skill showing both in the lighting, the focus, and the arrangement of the component parts. Several had titles describing what they were of or intended to convey.

In some pictures she was clothed, others, nearly naked. In one shot she could see the hint of a nipple, but none of the pictures were crude in showing her nudity. Given how often she'd seduced Alex by posing for him, shedding one article of clothing after another, it was amazing how few shots there were of her without clothes.

Maybe Alex didn't want others to see her naked? Chloe pondered that thought, its meaning giving a boost to her hopes. If he felt that way, maybe he cared for her more than she'd thought, cared enough to be jealous.

He hadn't liked her going out with others, even Nina. When she'd been late coming back from the park after meeting Pan, he'd acted quite concerned that she might have been with another man.

She turned another page. More pictures of her, out in the woods. One of the pictures looked like her statue at the museum. Alex had had her mimic the statue's pose, peering from behind a tree. He'd even included a picture of the statue for reference. Underneath it was a title, "nymph in the woods." She'd looked like a wood nymph, to be sure—Chloe smiled at the whimsy of it. She hadn't realized that Alex could see the humor in something like that.

More pictures of her. Some had been taken candidly, when he'd come up on her unawares. One was of her intent expression on getting the placement of a garnish just right for her last class project. Another showed her relaxing in the bath, with plenty of bubbles providing modesty, her face holding a blissful smile.

Bubble baths. Yes, that was another thing Chloe would miss.

One of the final photos made her gasp in surprise. He must have taken it after he'd returned from work, while she was asleep in bed. It was black and white, her hair a pale shimmer on the pillow, one arm carelessly flung above her head. The blanket molded to her body, but one of her legs had freed itself from the covers and lay on top of the sheet. Her face in sleep held peace and contentment, a hint of a smile on her lips. Dreaming maybe, of someone special.

A beautiful picture, to be sure. But that wasn't what surprised her. All of Alex's pictures were wonderful. But the caption on this one was "love dreaming".

Chloe closed the book and replaced it back on the bookcase where she'd found it. "Love dreaming", that's what he'd called one of her pictures. Alex never used the word love if he could help it. He didn't trust it, didn't trust those who used it too freely. That was one of the reasons she hadn't been able to tell him how she felt. But now he'd used the word, if only to label a photograph. It was a sign of how close they'd come.

She doubted even now he'd be able to use the word openly. In a week, maybe two, maybe in a month he would've been able to say it. He would have told her directly how he felt. He would have told her he loved her. But he just wasn't ready yet.

So close, so very, very close. Tears welled up in her eyes and she broke down. She gave in to her misery, letting them flow freely, not bothering to cover up her unhappiness. Heavy sobs robbed her of her breath and she gasped loudly. There was no one to hear her cry, no one to be silent for.

After a while she ran out of tears, although her sadness remained. She moved to the kitchen, grabbing a kitchen towel to wipe her face. What would Alex say if he found her crying like this? Maybe he'd grab his camera and take another picture. He could label this one, "love's despair".

Or maybe he wouldn't take a picture. Maybe he'd take her in his arms and hold her tight, promise her he'd make it all right, whatever the problem was. He might caress her back and kiss away her tears.

He might even tell her that he loved her.

Hope mingled with her despair. Maybe the goddess was wrong. It might not be too late. Alex would be home soon and she'd be able to talk to him about the picture. She'd remind him of how he never used the word love unless he meant it. It would be the perfect opportunity to ask him directly if he did love her.

He'd have to answer her, and the answer would have to be yes. If he'd labeled her his love, even if only through the caption on a picture, then he must mean it.

If he became evasive, there was something else she could do. She would tell him the truth. She would tell him she loved him, tonight. No more hints as to how she felt. Even if he still felt uncertain, he would see how things stood between them. Better to be open now.

He'd said he didn't trust those who use the word lightly. She'd have to convince him that she meant it.

All she needed was a little time. Maybe the goddess could help her, give her a little longer as a human. It was a spell after all, and Aphrodite was a powerful goddess. She could find a way to extend Chloe's time. It wasn't like she was asking for a miracle—just a couple weeks longer. Maybe if she prayed?

She bent her head. "Please mighty goddess, fairest of the fair. I know you see me now. Can't you help me? Give me the time I need to show Alex that what he feels for me is real."

Chloe opened her eyes and waited. No answer came, no whirlwind in the living room, no bright flash of light to announce the goddess's arrival. Only silence.

A wry smile crossed Chloe's face. *Figures.* The goddess did as she pleased, as was her prerogative. It didn't mean she wouldn't help, but she wouldn't make a guest appearance to do it.

The lump of dough on the counter caught her attention, bulging nicely under the damp cloth covering it. It looked close to ready. With one hand, Chloe pulled the cloth away, revealing the symmetrical loaf. It certainly looked ready. She'd just do a finger test to check how much it had risen. Still holding the cloth with her left hand, she poked the dough with her right.

Her finger went right through the dough as if it wasn't there.

Chloe snatched her hand back and stared at it. It tingled, but otherwise looked fine. She stared at the lump of dough. The surface was still smooth and shiny. There was no sign she'd poked her finger into it.

Trembling, Chloe tried to touch the counter. Again her fingers passed through it, although when she got to where they joined her palm, she felt some resistance. Dropping the towel, she used her other hand to explore the right. While she could see her fingers, her left hand was unable to feel them, only finding solidity when she reached the palm. She traced her hand and discovered she had about half of her thumb. No, wait. She tried again and only a third of her thumb was there.

The tingling from where her fingers should be became more pronounced and spread slowly into her palm. She tried again and this time couldn't find any sign of the thumb she could plainly see.

Fear turning her gut into knots, Chloe sought one of the kitchen stools, grateful for its firmness under her still-solid ass. An odd thought occurred to her. *She'd wanted to lose a little weight. Looks like she was going to lose all of it.* She tried not to laugh at that. A little laughter now could quickly become hysterical as her panic kicked in.

She was becoming unsubstantial again, losing her human body a little at a time. When she'd been a spirit, she'd been able to turn herself solid for short periods of time and as she returned to her spirit state, she'd felt the same tingling now coming from her right hand.

The spell Aphrodite had used to turn her human must be breaking up, just as the goddess had predicted. There would be no reprieve, no delay in her returning to her old state. Time had run out.

She stared at her right hand, noting that she could no longer feel the outer edges of the palm. Why it had started there, and why it was progressing so slowly she didn't understand, but was grateful for it. At the rate she was going, she'd be nothing but vapor within the hour. She had time to get back to the museum, if she started now. She had to be there in time to merge with her statue, otherwise she could very well lose herself in the spirit would.

She'd been there before and never wanted to go back. Better to be trapped inside a statue than drifting in formless space.

A glance at the clock told her it was still too early for Alex to get home. She couldn't wait for him. If he came in time, he could drive her to the museum. But what if he was late? Chloe resisted the urge to panic. That wasn't going to help her now. She'd have to get to the museum by herself. It was a walk, but not a long one. She'd be there in thirty minutes. Hopefully there would still be enough of her left to open the door so she'd be able to get in.

Horror filled her. She'd have to leave without saying goodbye. What would Alex think when he came and found her gone? Would he assume she'd left like Melody had, or would he understand that she'd had no choice? She'd promised to tell him why she was going.

She could leave a note to explain where she was. Maybe he'd come in time and would meet her there. Chloe grabbed one of her shopping lists and turned it over to the blank side. One problem, she'd learned to write with her right hand and only her left still had fingers to grip. The pen felt awkward and the letters she wrote hard to make out.

Controlling her fear and frustration, she did the best she could, taking long precious moments. To her the note was hard to read, barely legible but she didn't have time to try again. She left it on the counter next to the unbaked bread. Maybe he'd see that as part of the message, that her leaving had been unexpected and there were things she'd still meant to do.

Things like making his dinner, baking him bread, and telling him that she loved him. If she got the chance at the museum, she'd do the latter there.

With barely controlled sob, Chloe grabbed her coat and small purse and headed for the door. She had a long walk in front of her.

* * * * *

Where the hell was Chloe? After arriving home and not seeing her in the front part of the apartment, Alex had checked the bathroom and the bedroom to find no trace of her. Now he stood in the kitchen staring into the refrigerator, holding an unopened bottle of beer.

Some sort of casserole was on one of the shelves, while a bowl of salad waited on another. Obviously she was going to cook dinner. Funny thing, though. Normally by now the casserole would be in the oven.

As would the bread. Alex turned and stared again at the puffy lump of dough sitting on the countertop. Chloe didn't leave dough like that. She kept it covered with a cloth like…that one! He found the damp cloth lying on the kitchen floor. Alex put his bottle down and bent over to pick it up. He placed it in the sink.

Something was wrong, very, very wrong. Chloe would never have left a wet cloth on the floor. She wouldn't leave her dough uncovered and she would have started dinner by now.

Where was Chloe?

He looked again at the mute lump of dough, wishing it could tell him what had happened. Then his gaze fell on a piece of paper on the counter. He snatched it up. On one side was Chloe's neat handwriting, a shopping list. Milk, rice, eggs, grape leaves… What did she want grape leaves for?

The writing on the other side did not look like her handwriting at all. He could make out the first word, "Alex". Was the next one "darling"? It was hard to say. There were skips and jumps in the ink, as if she'd had trouble controlling the pen. Also the letters sloped to the wrong side. Had something happened to her hand?

He glanced wildly over at the knives in the rack. None were missing, and he saw no blood. If there had been an accident, would she have stopped to clean up the mess before leaving for the doctor?

The uneasy feeling creeping about in his stomach turned into a solid lump of fear. Chloe was gone and he didn't think it was by her own choice. Other than the note, he had no way of knowing where she was.

Foregoing his beer, Alex sat down at the table to try and puzzle out the note. He made out another word, "sorry." Sorry for what, that she had left? What was she sorry for?

The "C" at the bottom was probably her signature. Alex breathed a faint sigh of relief. At least he knew the note was from her. But what did it say? He stared at it again, this time focusing on the letters right above the "C". These were less shaky and not quite so run together. She must have taken more care with them. He could make out an "I" and an "l". Next were "o", and a "v", then "e" and "y". The final letters were "o" and "u".

He sat up and stared at the wall. It was a blank wall, in an unattractive color. Chloe had wanted to paint it, but he'd said no, not wanting to spend the money...why was he thinking of this now?

Because it was easier to think about how often he'd disappointed her than about the note. He'd given her enough reasons to leave and fewer reasons to stay. Alex returned to the note and reread the last three words. Even though there were no spaces between the words, he knew there were three words because there was only one thing she'd be saying with those letters.

He rested his head on the tabletop, knowing he'd lost his chance. She'd told him weeks ago she might have to leave suddenly, but he'd expected to have more time. There was no more time.

Chloe had written "I love you". That wasn't something she'd write lightly. She wasn't a coward like he was. She'd have spoken the words before leaving them in a note. He glanced over at the photo album on the bookshelf. Had she even seen it before she'd left?

But she had written the words, and that could mean only one thing. She'd written them because she knew she was leaving and wouldn't be back. Chloe was gone.

Loss and despair hit him hard, and he fought the urge to give in to tears. Twice now he'd fallen in love, and twice he'd lost her. The difference this time was that now he deserved it. Chloe deserved better than him, a man too afraid to admit he had feelings for her. Maybe leaving was a good thing for her.

A noise from the living room alerted him that he was no longer alone. He looked up just as a woman with closely cropped dark hair appeared, carrying a guitar case.

A guitar case? "You looking for the Von Trapp family? I think you have the wrong address."

Her eyes narrowed and Alex immediately regretted his joke. This woman didn't look like she liked him very much.

"You must be Alex. I'm looking for Chloe."

"Yeah, I'm Alex." He checked out her outfit, tight blue jeans and a low-cut sweater that must have cost a fortune, and made an educated guess. "You must be her sister, Nina."

He nodded at the case. "You have more sex toys in there?"

She ignored his question. "Where is Chloe?"

Alex shook his head. "I don't know. Gone, I think."

"Gone?" Nina looked upset. "Where did she go? Did she say?"

"She was gone when I got home. I found a note." He held it out. "It's hard to make out, maybe you can read it."

Just before she took it, he remembered the last few words and snatched it away. He could tell just by looking at her that Nina was a real bitch, and the last thing he wanted was to share his love's sweet words with her.

Nina dropped the case and glared at him. "Are you going to show it to me or not?"

Shaking his head, Alex folded the paper and put it in his pocket. "They were private words. For me."

She arched one eyebrow. "I thought you couldn't read them?"

"I could some. The ones that mattered."

"Oh?" Something like a smile crossed Nina's face. "I guess that means she finally decided to tell you that she was nuts about you."

"You knew?" How could his sweet Chloe have told this woman about how she felt, when she'd never told him? Oh, but she'd been afraid to tell him, and this woman strange as it might seem, was Chloe's sister. Of course she'd told her sister.

Hope rose in him. Maybe she'd told her sister something else, like where she'd gone. "Do you know where she went?"

His hope died when she shook her head. "I know where she should have gone, but she probably didn't. Are you sure I can't look at the note?"

What the hell. She looked at least as lost as he was. He pulled it from his pocket and handed it to her.

Nina squinted at the ill-formed letters. "Huh, looks like she wrote this with her left hand. It is hard to read, but

I think I understand it. She had to go, it was sudden, and…and… And she wants you to meet her at the museum!" she finished triumphantly.

"The museum?" Alex glanced at the clock. "It will be closed in five minutes."

"You have a key, right?"

"Sure. But why would she need to go to the museum?"

"Because that's where her statue is. She has to go back into it."

"What? Why?"

"Because…" Her voice trailed off for a moment and she didn't look him in the eye. Alex wondered what she was hiding. "Let's just say that the spell that made her human has failed and if she doesn't get back to her statue, she'll wind up nothing but a loose spirit again."

"The spell failed? How come? That was Aphrodite's spell, how could it fail?"

"I can't tell you, Alex. Maybe you should ask the goddess that?"

Oh yeah. Like he'd take the goddess on. She'd scared the crap out of him when he'd met her at the museum the first time. Still, if she had answers for him, he might ask her. He needed to know what was going on and why Chloe had left him.

She hadn't wanted to. Her note had told him that with the illegible "I love you." Now he needed to know what it was that was making the spell fail and why she needed to return to her statue. Maybe he'd be able to fix things so she could stay with him. He needed her to stay with him.

He needed that a lot. "You're saying she's at the museum." Sudden hope rose. Maybe it wasn't too late to fix things. Alex jumped to his feet and headed for his coat and the door, determination in his stride.

"Wait for me," Nina called, grabbing her guitar case.

He glared at it. "You won't need that. We aren't going to a folk-sing, you know."

She clutched the case to her chest and narrowed her eyes. "I come and it comes...understand?"

It was too much trouble to argue. "Have it your way. The back's filled with junk so you'll have to carry it on your lap. Fortunately there isn't much to you so it shouldn't be too bad."

He held the door for her and slammed it on his way out.

Chapter Sixteen

By the time Chloe reached the service entrance to the museum, she could barely feel her right arm past her elbow. If she bent her arm, it went right through the fabric of her sweatshirt and coat, which continued to hang straight down. Having a naked arm poking through the fabric of her garments was too strange to look at so she let the arm remain straight so it continued to be covered by her clothes.

A revolting development. Her clothes would probably fall off her once her body lacked the solidity to support them. She'd end up naked before she could join with her statue unless some small amount of her magic returned to her so she could manufacture a decent garment.

At least the tingle wasn't uncomfortable, nor was her arm cold, despite the frigid temperature outside. It could freeze tonight, she thought. A good night to indulge in the luxury of staying snuggled under the bedcovers with someone you loved.

That was a luxury she'd never have again.

Chloe suppressed a quick sob, fighting to control her tears. It was hard enough to leave without torturing herself with images of what she was leaving behind. Worried that she might have to find another way in, she tried the door and found it unlocked. She let out the breath she'd been holding.

After one last look around and a deep breath of fresh outdoor air, Chloe slipped inside.

The dimly lit service corridor stretched before her. Cautiously she moved into the building, hoping to avoid notice. The practice of many nights when she'd slipped from her statue to explore the museum returned to her. No one had ever caught her during those adventures.

Well, no one until Alex had caught her that is. She'd need to be extra careful tonight. The museum was closed and it wasn't likely that the staff would approve of her presence. She had to get to her statue before she finished dematerializing.

From somewhere up ahead came voices. Chloe flattened herself against the wall, knowing she'd be spotted if they came this way. Fortunately she heard the voices grow faint and disappear. So far her luck was holding. The door had been unlocked and no one had spotted her. Carefully she made her way to the gallery where her statue was kept. Once there, she could relax a little. She'd easily be able to hide in one of the deep window niches until things were quiet. That close to her statue, she wouldn't have a problem slipping back inside when the spell that kept her human failed.

The gallery she wanted should be just to the left. Chloe made the turn and entered past the huge Grecian urns that guarded either side of the entrance. She passed several statuary groups, heading for the center. It should be just ahead.

It wasn't.

Chloe stared at the empty space where for long, long years her statue had stood. There was no sign of it, no marble base, no truncated tree, no figure of a wood nymph peeking from behind the trunk. Was she in the wrong place? She moved closer and noticed the paleness of the marble floor where the base should have been. It had been here.

Could they have moved it? Alex hadn't said anything but perhaps he didn't know. Tamping down her desperation, she searched the gallery and took a brief look at the one next to it. No sign of it, anywhere.

Trembling, Chloe sank onto a marble bench. Where could it have gone? The goddess had told her to get to the statue as soon as she felt something change. If she wasn't near it, she'd evaporate into mist as soon as she lost the last of her solid shape. She'd become lost, a mere spirit on the wind as she had been a long time ago.

It sounded like a romantic fate, but it wasn't. At least with her statue she could become solid occasionally and be able to see and experience some form of life. Not as much as she wanted—but what she wanted she couldn't have anyway.

A tear trickled down her face, followed by another. At least at this point she could still cry. Chloe bent her head into her hands and gave into despair. "Oh, great goddess Aphrodite. What am I going to do?"

"You still pray to her?" A familiar voice drew her attention to the corner of the room. Leaning against one of the pillars was Pan, arms folded over his bare chest, his hairy legs crossed at the ankle. As always he was virtually naked, only a loincloth hiding his genitals, and that not all that effectively. Beneath the fabric a bulge appeared that grew more pronounced the longer he stared at her.

He shook his head at her. "Chloe, haven't you learned by now who your real friends are?"

Chloe narrowed her eyes at him. "I wouldn't call you a friend, Pan."

"Really?" His hurt look might have fooled her if it hadn't been for the amused glint in his eyes. "But I'm here to help you. Honest."

"There is nothing honest about you." With a nod of her head, she indicated the empty space where her statue should have been. "You wouldn't know where it went, would you?"

"What are you talking about? Did you misplace something?"

"I misplaced nothing. Someone stole my statue!"

"Stole it?" Pan grinned. "Not at all. I borrowed for a little while, that's all."

"Borrowed? How do you 'borrow' a statue?"

"When one is a god, one can do many things. I was struck by how much the figure looked like you and since I couldn't have the real thing, I simply borrowed the statue so I could make a copy of it."

Chloe didn't believe him for a moment. "You just happened to borrow it on the one night I needed it?"

He shrugged his shoulders. "Funny how things work sometimes."

"Very funny. Could you bring it back? Please?" Chloe tramped down on her panic. She could feel very little of her right arm now, but she didn't want to let Pan know how desperate she was.

"No," he said slowly. "But I could take you to it."

Take her to it? "Where is it, Pan? In your bedroom?"

"Echo, what do you take me for? I told you I wouldn't force you into my bed. Your statue is quite safe, in the garden of my home."

He was good. If she didn't know better she'd guess that his outrage was real. Chloe rested her left hand on her shoulder and tried not to think about how little of her right arm existed below her shoulder.

Pan approached. For the first time she saw honest concern in his face. "What is it, little one?" He pointed to her arm. "Is there something wrong?"

What was the use of hiding it? Maybe he'd take pity on her and bring her statue back. "The spell Aphrodite used to make me human is breaking up." She pulled off her coat and held up her right hand. It appeared ghost-like in the dim light of the museum. "I'm losing substance, becoming just a spirit again."

Pan reached for Chloe's transparent hand and to her surprise, captured it in his. She felt his fingers close around her palm, warm and sensual, and under his fingers the transparency disappeared. He used one finger to stroke her arm and where he touched, the skin grew solid.

She looked up at him in astonishment. "I can feel your touch."

A crooked smile grew across his face, and for the first time Pan seemed less the god of lechery, and more someone Chloe might actually want to know. In spite of herself, Chloe returned his smile with one of her own.

He raised her hand to his lips and kissed it gently. "Did you not believe me when I said I could help you? I can replace the spell the goddess used and bring you back to immortality. I can give you back your life, Echo."

Pan stood too close to her now. She smelled his scent,

flooding her nose. His musky essence had been described as being able to drive the most chaste vestal virgin into opening her legs and begging for a good fucking. Chloe was hardly virginal or chaste, and while his aroma didn't appeal to her the way Alex's did, she couldn't help but be aroused by it.

She put her hand on his chest, feeling the coarse manly hair, so different from the fleece of his legs. It was easy to imagine her breasts buried in that hair as he lay over her, pounding that donkey-sized cock of his into her pussy.

In spite of herself, Chloe felt her panties dampen in instant sympathy with her thoughts. "Pan, I don't know..."

Grasping her by the elbows, Pan pulled her to her feet. He dragged her closer into his arms, tight against his chest, his face inches from hers. "What don't you know, little Echo? What I want? What you want? Let me show you, then."

His mouth came down hard on hers, a powerful kiss, masterful. It was the kiss of someone who knew just what he wanted and how to get it, a kiss of claiming. It should have rocked her off her feet and turned her into a puddle.

Except that it didn't. Chloe felt...very little. She tried to participate, opening her mouth to give his tongue access, but that didn't improve things. It wasn't like he was doing something wrong. It was a very nice kiss. But something about it felt wrong and it just didn't put her in the mood.

Pan pulled back and stared down at her, his eyes showing the same surprise she felt. His sensual lips pulled down into a deep frown, reflecting disapproval over her lack of reaction. "Don't you like being kissed?"

"Yes, of course," she said slowly. "I don't know what's wrong."

Her not responding bothered him. He shook his head. "You're probably just overcome with the situation. Worry about your arm, about your future." Pan spoke decisively, as if trying to convince himself. "It will be better later, when we're alone."

He glanced around. "Besides, this isn't the most romantic place for a first kiss."

It was just outside this hallway that she and Alex had shared their first kiss, and that had been romantic enough, she recalled. Not that she'd tell Pan that. She shivered at the memory of how Alex's lips had touched hers, igniting desires she'd long ago forgotten she had. Unlike Pan's kiss, nice as it had been, Alex's kiss had turned her to flame.

She didn't even feel remotely warm in the god's arms.

Pan released her and she realized that even without him touching it, her right arm hadn't disappeared again. At least she was in one piece now.

"Come with me, Echo, to Olympus. Your statue is there, at my home, in my garden. That is a more fitting place for our talk. You may return to the stone if you want, I won't stop you. All I ask is a chance to show you that there is more to life than falling in love with a human man and giving up your natural divinity. It's been a long time since you've been with the immortals and tasted our life. Give yourself a chance to experience it again before you make your decision. I'll not take anything not willingly given. That's my promise."

She could hear the sincerity in his voice and see

honesty in his face. Pan was many things, but not a liar or a cheat. He'd taken her statue, but promised she could return to it if she wanted. Perhaps she should go with him.

Chloe made her decision. She put one hand on his chest. "Okay, Pan, I'll go with you on one condition."

He grinned at her obviously thinking that he'd won. "Anything!"

"Call me Chloe. That's my name now."

A contemptuous look came across his face. "The name the human gave you? Why should I use that?"

Summoning her courage, Chloe raised her eyes to meet his. "Because it is my wish that you do so, Pan. I asked for a new name and got one, so use it, please."

Pan grumbled under his breath and Chloe was just able to make out the words. "Aphrodite said you'd say something like that."

"Very well," he said in a normal voice. "Chloe, would you please come with me to my home on Olympus?" He gave her a gracious bow, with only a hint of mockery in it, holding out his hand to her.

Chloe nodded her head in return. "I'll be happy to, Pan," she said and took his hand.

Pan flicked his fingers and the room grayed around them, the preparation for the jump to Olympus, the gods' dominion. Pan put his arms around her and Chloe braced herself. She didn't see Alex and Nina enter the room just before the world winked out completely.

* * * * *

"Chloe!" Alex cried as she disappeared, but she didn't turn to acknowledge him or give any indication that she'd heard him call her name.

Gone! Chloe was gone, disappeared. She hadn't waited for him to catch up with her as she'd asked in the note. Worse, she hadn't been alone, but had been held in the arms of another man.

She'd left her coat on one of the benches. Alex lifted it and held it close. It was still warm and smelled of her light scent. Despair hit hard, and he sank onto the bench.

He looked over at Nina, still carrying her ridiculous guitar case. "She's gone. What can I do?"

She shook her head and for a moment Alex thought he saw sympathy in her eyes.

"That was Pan with her. We talked to him before and he'd offered to help save her if she..." her voice trailed off and she coughed once, as if to clear her throat. "Well, anyway, she seems to be with Pan. That's good since he can fix the spell she's under."

Alex's hope rose. "Fix it? You mean he can keep her from going back into the statue?"

"Well sort of." Nina hedged. "He'll keep her from being a spirit, but he wants her to be a nymph again. She won't be a mortal woman anymore."

Not a mortal woman? But then... "You mean she won't be able to stay with me?"

"She could if she wanted to, at least for a while. But nymphs have rules they have to follow and they can't stay on Earth for long periods. She'd have to leave you eventually."

She'd leave him eventually. He'd expected that anyway. After all, Chloe didn't really belong with him. It had been a fluke that she'd wound up in his arms and turned human. She hadn't really wanted that. All she'd wanted was a bit of sex, same as he had and it had gotten out of hand. That's all. He'd taken her in because she'd had no place else to go once she'd turned human.

So what if it had been the best accident to ever befall him? Had it been the same for her? Wasn't her returning to her former state as a nymph a good thing? She wouldn't grow old and she'd never die. She'd always be beautiful and young. So full of life and laughter.

So full of love. And none of it for him. He couldn't stand that.

He looked up at Nina, still watching him with her intense eyes. "What can I do, Nina?"

"Why should you do anything? She's in good hands with Pan."

"Because I want to. I need to." He took a deep breath. "I want...that is, I need her back."

One of her rare smiles curved her lips. "You need Chloe back? As a human?"

Alex set his jaw. "I know it's selfish of me. She'd be better off as one of you, better off as a nymph. But I can't help it. I want her back, Nina. I need her with me. Otherwise..."

Nina held up one hand. "Spare me the rest, human. Chloe is the one to hear it, not me." A grudging respect shone in her eyes. "There might be more to you than I expected." She reached out to him with her free hand. "All right, I can get us both to Olympus and we'll find them there. Take my hand and close your eyes. Transfer can be a little disorienting if you aren't used to it."

Still holding Chloe's coat, Alex stood. Heart pounding, he took Nina's hand. It was cool and soft on his palm. As she'd instructed, he closed his eyes.

"Start counting, Alex, and don't stop until you reach ten."

He did as she asked. The light through his closed eyes was a dim glow.

"One, two, three..."

The light outside his eyes faded to black and he felt a jerk in the pit of his stomach. For a moment, he couldn't feel Nina's hand in his, or the rest of his body.

"...seven, eight..."

His body returned, as did the light. Alex took a deep breath. "...nine, ten."

Alex opened his eyes and gaped at his surroundings. It was if he'd been transported back to ancient Greece. They'd materialized in a small open temple-like building on top of a high hill.

Around him stood tall, carved marble pillars, supporting a roof of stone. The interior of the roof was painted blue to mimic the sky and held small stars and a slender crescent moon. The ceiling reminded him of Chloe's earrings.

Down the hill he saw many buildings with similar characteristics, stone roofs and walls, sometimes fronted by stone pillars. Narrow streets set with stone wound down between the houses, separating them. The marble gleamed in rose-colored hues from the sun setting beyond the distant hills.

Chuckling came from behind him and he turned to see Nina watching his reaction to his new surroundings.

She grinned. "Welcome to Olympus, human."

"Where are we?"

"Olympus? It's a kind of alternative reality, home to the gods and minor mythological individuals you've heard stories about. This is the main Olympian transfer station. I can't transfer directly to my home, or to Pan's place. I don't have enough power so I had to bring us here first," she told him apologetically. "It's just a short walk now."

He had to find Chloe before she decided to become a nymph forever, and time was getting short. "Fine, we'll walk. You lead the way."

Nina hoisted her guitar case higher in her arms and took off down the hill. Tossing Chloe's coat over his shoulder, Alex followed close behind.

Chapter Seventeen

In the setting sun, the color of her statue was all roses and pinks. It had never looked so beautiful before as it did sitting in Pan's garden. What a shame that it had to go back into the museum.

That was one fault with returning to the stone. She'd be stuck indoors all day. The sun's warmth touched her face and she filled her lungs with the garden's air, perfumed by the flowers and the fresh grass forming a carpet under her feet. Back on Earth the time had been winter, but here it was late springtime.

It was always late spring on Olympus. Chloe settled onto one of Pan's garden chairs, appreciating that it was made of springy willow wood and not cold marble. Pan was the god of nature and his garden home reflected that. Flowering plants grew in wild abandon, not trimmed into unnatural formal forms but gently shaped to follow the contours of the overgrown flowerbeds. All the furnishings, including the chair she sat on and table nearby, were natural objects manufactured by the plants themselves to serve Pan.

Around the edges of the space, bushes had grown together to form screens that provided privacy and in one corner a group of small trees created a secluded bower, which held Pan's bedroom.

Chloe eyed the opening to the bower uneasily. While she'd never been in there, she knew its reputation. More than one nymph had returned from Pan's bower in happy disarray and with stories to tell. The god had stamina, imagination, and the equipment to fulfill any nymph's fantasies. Those who hadn't been invited to Pan's bed dreamed of the day they would be.

Now Chloe sat where so many of those nymphs had wanted to be, and all she wanted was to go home. She didn't want Pan's expertise—she wanted Alex's warm, sweet, and sometimes clumsy touch.

"Would you like some refreshments, Chloe?"

She turned to tell him no, and her jaw dropped. Pan had changed, now wearing a short tunic that belted at the waist instead his loincloth, but it wasn't just his clothes that were different. Gone were the fleece-covered legs and the hooves. Instead, strong man legs stretched to a pair of sandal-clad feet. She peered up at his curly sandy-brown hair and noticed the tiny horns were gone. Even his beard was closer trimmed, less wild in appearance. Instead of the god of nature, he now looked like a normal and devastatingly handsome young man.

He noticed her stare and smiled with a little embarrassment. "I thought this might make you more comfortable. You've become used to a human appearance."

Chloe's face heated. "It wasn't how you looked that bothered me, Pan."

He shrugged and headed for the cool spring in one corner. From the water he pulled a basket and earthenware pitcher, then from a small woven cabinet attached to the side of a tree, collected goblets. He brought all back to her, setting them on the wicker table.

The basket held grapes, ripe and icy-cold from the spring, and the pitcher a crystal-clear amber wine chilled to perfection. The simple stoneware goblets were exquisitely shaped, as were the basket and pitcher. The gods certainly knew how to live well.

Pan poured wine for them both and raised his glass. "To new beginnings. May we both find what we want tonight."

Chloe doubted that what she wanted was the same as Pan, but she drank anyway. So far the god had been a perfect host.

The wine tasted crisp and cold on her tongue, a perfect complement for the sweetness of the grapes. To her surprise, Chloe was hungrier than she'd thought as she nibbled several small bunches of the delectable globules.

Pan laughed as she reached for a fourth cluster. "You certainly have an appetite, Chloe. I wonder, does that extend to all things or just your stomach?" He reached over to caress her hand. "I look forward to finding out."

The grapes she held dropped onto the table. "You said you'd let me return to my statue if I wanted to."

He folded his hands and stared at her. "Can you honestly say that is what you want? You eat and drink with too much enthusiasm for someone willing to give up her life. Can you really return to feeling nothing, to being no more than a shadow in the world?"

Chloe toyed with her goblet, feeling the slightly rough texture under her fingers. Such an exquisite sensation, to be able to feel. She could imagine it was Alex's face she touched, rough with his morning beard.

She didn't have to give it up. If she gave in to Pan, she'd remain alive, able to touch, to taste, able to breathe fragrant air like that of his garden.

She'd even be able to love Alex if he took her back after she'd had sex with Pan. It wasn't impossible that he would. After all, she'd had no choice. Would Alex really hold it against her?

Of course she'd be a nymph and she'd been told that human men couldn't resist minor divinities, but that hadn't been her experience. Narcissus hadn't had a bit of trouble resisting her.

Of course, Nick was now hopelessly devoted to Violet. She remembered the look in his eyes when she'd watched the pair making love at the museum. If only she'd seen that look in Alex's eyes, or heard the kind of soft words Nick had spoken from her own love's lips.

Why did she have to have fallen in love with Alex? It made everything so complicated.

She looked up to see Pan's serious regard. "What are you thinking about, Chloe? Your human lover?"

No point in lying to a god. Chloe nodded. "I'm not sure I can forget him, Pan."

"I'm not asking you to." A disgruntled frown appeared on the god's face. He pushed his goblet away with an impatient gesture. "I'm not used to taking a woman who thinks of another. What does this Alex have that I don't?"

My heart, she wanted to tell him. Instead she chose silence as her answer.

Pan stood and pulled her to her feet and into his arms. His hands were warm around her waist and his massive erection made a dent in her belly. She gazed up into his intense brown eyes. They were the same color as Alex's and yet not the same. How could two pairs of eyes be so different?

Pan's brown eyes narrowed in irritation. "You still think of him, don't you? Let's see if this takes him off your mind." Pan closed his mouth over hers in a demanding kiss. His hands kneaded her bottom, lifting her tight against his throbbing cock while he devoured her mouth.

It was enough to take any woman's breath away. Unfortunately, it only made Chloe lightheaded from lack of oxygen as the kiss lasted longer than her stored air. She gasped when he finally let her breathe.

Now the brown eyes showed complete bewilderment. "What is the matter with you woman? Is there something wrong with me?" He readjusted his hold lifting her onto the table and spreading her legs so he could fit between them. Now his cock rubbed against her open crotch. The pressure against her clit finally woke it up and it throbbed into awareness. Chloe moaned in response.

"That's more like it," Pan said, satisfaction in his tone. He leaned forward, intending to kiss her. "Now let's try this again."

"Let's not!"

Chloe turned at the sound of Alex's voice. He and Nina stood by the gate to the street. Alex looked furious and Nina was holding a guitar case.

A guitar case? What was going on here? She pulled against Pan's arms, and he released her.

Chloe saw her coat across Alex's shoulders. He dropped in on the grass and folded his arms across his chest. "So this is why you left me, to be with him?"

"No Alex, I didn't want to." Her voice faltered. "I didn't have any choice."

"No choice? Because of the immortality he can give you?" He seemed to deflate a little. "I thought...I read your note."

Her note, the one that said "I love you"? Chloe's hopes soared. Maybe Alex did love her and would declare himself before it was too late.

Pan grabbed her, one arm around her waist, his hold possessive. He glared at the others. "What are you doing here? Nemesis, what made you bring this human to my home?"

Her sister shrugged. "He wanted to come. Said he had something to say to Chloe before she went back into her statue."

"She's not going back," Pan said. "She gives herself to me and I'll make her a nymph again."

Alex broke in. "I don't want her to be a nymph. I want her to be a woman."

"You care what happens to her? Truly?" The god scoffed.

"Of course I care." Alex stepped forward. "Let her go."

Chloe twisted away from Pan. Jumping from the table she ran to Alex, throwing her arms around him. Her left arm landed against his back, but the right went clear through his body.

She jumped back and stared at her hand. It was transparent once more. "No!" she moaned. "The spell is failing again."

Alex reached for her arm, his eyes wide as his hand went through it. "It's like you were before, when you were in the statue."

She stared up at him. "I have to go back into it, Alex. The spell Aphrodite gave me is failing. If I don't, I could wind up a loose spirit and be lost forever."

Alex grasped her left shoulder still solid under his hand. "What can we do, Chloe?" He turned to Pan. "You can help her, right?"

The god's sardonic smile gave him a devilish appearance, even in his human form. "I could. She knows what the price is."

Alex stepped in front of her. "You'd force her to sleep with you?"

"Sleeping wasn't what I had in mind, but sex is the price of my help."

"What kind of a man—or god—gets his rocks off this way, compelling a woman into his bed?" Alex's contemptuous tone raked through the air and Pan's face darkened in response.

"Perhaps there is another way," the god said ominously, stroking his short beard with one hand. "Would you fight me for her? A little wrestling match perhaps? You pin me and I'll help her."

Alex stepped forward, clenching his fists. "Anytime."

"Alex, no!" Chloe stared at the pair, the human-looking god and her beloved offering to fight to save her. What was Alex doing? Pan was a *god*, for Hades sake.

She grabbed his arm. "Alex, he'll kill you."

"I won't let you return to the statue, and I won't let him fuck you. If that means I fight him, then I fight him."

She tried to hold him back, but he easily broke the hold of her one arm. The two men faced off in the middle of the grassy yard, Pan exuding confidence, Alex showing no fear, only determination in his face. If it weren't for the fact that he was behaving like an idiot, she would've been proud of him.

Yes, he was six inches taller than the god, but that didn't make him stronger. Bigger wasn't better, not when your opponent could shapeshift if he chose.

Nina pulled on her left arm, and drew her away from the fight. "We better keep out of the way."

Chloe struggled ineffectually to break her grasp. "No, Nina. Alex will get hurt."

"Pan won't do more than give him a good lesson. Your human should know better than to challenge a god."

"Pan doesn't even look like a god right now. Alex doesn't know how strong he really is."

Nina chuckled. "He's about to find out, real fast."

The two men charged each other, coming together with the sound of two solid bodies hitting hard. Both men let out a grunt as their arms wrapped around each other's waist, struggling to pull the other to the ground. To her surprise, Alex actually held his own in this first round, feet planted firmly on the ground as Pan tried to pull him off-balance.

The god's eyes narrowed in consternation over his failure, but he didn't let up, simply changed his hold on Alex, slipping his hands up to the bigger man's shoulders. With almost practiced ease, Pan flipped Alex around, driving him to his knees onto the ground, one arm locked around Alex's neck.

He squeezed tight, cutting off Alex's air. "Give in, human."

Alex pulled ineffectually on Pan's arm. "I won't let you have her."

"It's her choice to make." Pan looked up and called to her. "What do you want, Chloe? Shall I break his neck, or will you serve me as I've asked?"

She stepped forward. "I'll do anything you want, Pan. Don't hurt him, please."

From the corner of her eye, Chloe saw a flash of dying sunlight on something metal. She glanced over to see Nina, armed with a bow, aiming a metal tipped arrow right at Alex's heart. The open guitar case lay abandoned on the ground nearby.

"No!" she screamed and snatched the arrow from her sister's grasp. She held it up to Nina's startled face. "How could you?"

She marched toward the two men, holding the arrow in her hand.

Nina called after her. "It's not what it seems, Chloe!"

Ignoring her, Chloe brandished the arrow in front of Pan. "Is this how you do things, Pan, using others to kill your rivals? You're a god, shouldn't you be acting like one? Using your power to get me into bed, tricking Alex into fighting you. And now this, getting Nina to shoot him." She tossed the arrow to the corner of the garden.

With a growl, Pan released Alex, taking a step back. He shook himself and the glamour fell off him, leaving him dressed in his usual loincloth, his horns and goat legs back in place. Alex's eyes widened at the god's appearance.

"I knew nothing of Nina's treachery. As for the other, I wouldn't have forced you into my bed. If you'd refused I'd have still remade you back into a nymph. I just wanted you to know your rightful place."

"My rightful place is with the man I love, Pan, even if he doesn't love me back."

Alex staggered to his feet and coughed once, then twice. "Who says I don't love you?" he said when he finally got his voice. "I've been nuts about you since you came to live with me." He held up his hands. "You think I'd let that screwball sister of yours drag me to an alternate reality so I could talk you into coming back if I didn't love you?"

Alex loved her? Chloe burst into tears and rushed into his arms, burying herself in his chest, feeling his warm strength hold her close. He kissed her forehead and the top of her head, his words lost in her hair.

Finally she had to know what he was saying. She pulled her face out of his shirt and gazed up. Alex chuckled, then pulled a handkerchief from his pocket and tenderly wiped her face.

"Chloe, babe, I'm going to have to work on keeping you from crying. You really are a mess when you cry."

"You really love me?"

He smiled and all the love she could hope for was in that smile. "With all my heart, babe."

There was still something wrong. Chloe still couldn't feel her right arm. "I don't understand. The goddess said that the spell was based on love, and would break if we didn't love each other. Why is my arm still gone?"

She turned to Pan. "Could you fix it again?"

He held up his hands. "What I did was temporary and it faded faster than I'd expected. This is Aphrodite's spell and I'm not going to interfere with it."

"Nice to hear that, Pan. Too bad it's a little too late."

From the corner of the garden Aphrodite appeared and from the expression on her face she wasn't any too happy.

Chapter Eighteen

"Doesn't anyone knock anymore?" Pan grunted in disgust, hands on his hips.

Ignoring him, Aphrodite glared at them. In one hand was the arrow Chloe had tossed away. As she watched, the goddess slapped it against her palm.

Chloe dropped to her knees. "Mighty goddess, please forgive us." Maybe a show of humility would make the goddess happy, or at least keep her from firing any lightning bolts at Alex or her. Nina and Pan could fend for themselves, especially Nina after she tried to kill Alex.

She tugged on Alex's hand, and reluctantly he knelt next to her. "Yeah, goddess. What Chloe said."

Chloe closed her eyes and hoped the goddess's sense of humor hadn't completely disappeared.

Aphrodite approached them, still holding the arrow. "Please stand up. It's hard to see your faces when you kneel like that."

Alex stood first and helped Chloe to her feet. She was still off-balance from the loss of her right arm.

Aphrodite tapped both of them on the head with the arrow. "I see that you two have finally declared your love. Excellent, I'm pleased with both of you. You have my blessing and wishes for a long happy life together. Lots of babies, I adore babies."

Alex cleared his throat. "About Chloe's arm, goddess. Could you fix it?"

For an instant the goddess seemed confused. "Her arm?"

Chloe held up her transparent limb and the goddess seemed to blush with embarrassment. "Oh, good heavens. I really need to work on that spell. It is forever doing something unexpected." She waved the arrow like a magic wand and immediately Chloe's arm returned to normal.

Chloe grasped Alex with her returned right hand. "Oh thank you, goddess."

She smiled beneficently at them. "My pleasure, children."

Aphrodite beckoned to Nina, who approached reluctantly. She pointed to the bow. "I believe that isn't something that belongs to you."

Looking sheepish, Nina handed the bow over to her. "I just borrowed it, goddess. I hadn't planned to keep it."

The goddess glared in response. "Borrowing an item like this without permission is a serious offense, Nina."

"But I didn't mean any harm...all I wanted..."

Aphrodite interrupted her. "You were interfering with my plans." She glanced over at Pan who was watching with increasing concern. "I've said before I won't stand for interference." She pointed to a part of the grass not too far from where Pan stood. "Stand over there."

Eyes wide, Nina moved to where the goddess was pointing. Her eyes widened further when Aphrodite fit the arrow into the bow and drew it back, taking deadly aim right at Nina's heart.

"Goddess, please," the nymph cried out.

"I told both you and Pan not to interfere with my plans, maybe this will teach you a lesson." She let fly the arrow.

"No!" With a shout, Pan jumped in front of Nina, the arrow piercing his back. He arched in agony as it tore through him, exiting through his chest to hit the nymph between the breasts. For a moment the pair stared at each other, pinned together by the arrow's shaft. Then the rod seemed to melt away and the arrowhead fell.

As the arrow disappeared Chloe realized what Nina had tried to do for her. "It was one of Eros' bows and arrows," she said softly. She stroked Alex's arm. "She wanted to make you love me."

Pan overheard her. He stared down into Nina's astonished face.

"You tried to save me?" she asked, her voice full of wonder.

"That was one of *Eros'* arrows?" he bellowed at the same time.

Both took a deep breath. Pan's eyes narrowed. "How could you be that stupid? Interfering with the goddess, stealing from Eros. Do you know what you've done? I've been hit with Eros' arrow when I was staring right at you. Now I'm going to be infatuated with you for gods know how long."

Nina's eyes narrowed in response. "No one told you to jump in the way, you big oaf. And for your information, that arrow hit me, too. You think I want you wanting me, or me wanting you? This is as bad for me as it is for you."

He stared down at her. "You're a mouthy little wench, aren't you? I probably ought to put that mouth of yours to work doing something useful for a change."

She glared up at him. "Oh, yeah? Like what?"

Seizing her shoulders, Pan pulled her into his arms and kissed her long and hard. As Chloe watched, Nina's knees buckled and she seemed to faint when he finally let her up for air.

Absolute satisfaction was in Pan's expression as he stared down at the swooning nymph. "That's more like it," Chloe heard him murmur as he threw the semiconscious Nina over his shoulder. He turned to face them. "Please show yourselves out. I've got something to attend to." Then he took long determined strides for his bower.

Alex stared after the god. "Did you see the size of that package? He must be as big as a horse."

"More like a donkey," Chloe told him and at his sharp glance she raised a placating hand. "Nina told me."

Just before they passed through the door, Nina lifted her head and Chloe saw a smile of sheer delight on her sister's face. She suppressed a giggle. It didn't look like her sister was as upset by this situation as she claimed.

Aphrodite clapped her hands, regaining their attention. "Well now," she said brightly. "I guess that wraps things up here. If you'll hold hands, I'll transfer you back to the museum."

Alex reclaimed her coat and helped her into it. "It's cold back there, you know."

"I know. But it will be spring soon."

He watched her face. "Nina told me it was always spring here. Are you sure you want to come back with me?"

Chloe took his hand with both of hers, holding it over her heart. "I know what I've done, Alex, what I've given up, and what I've gained in return. I'd rather have a few seasons with you than centuries alone."

He stroked her face lightly. "Come home with me, Chloe. I'll keep you warm, always." He covered her mouth with his, wrapping his arms around her back to support her when her knees buckled.

They were still kissing when Aphrodite waved her hands and sent the pair back to the museum.

Paying no attention to the odd cries now coming from the Pan's bower, Aphrodite stared around the garden. The empty guitar case she ignored, but she collected the silver arrowhead from where it had fallen. After passing through the god and hitting the nymph, it had transformed into the shape of a heart. *Pretty.* It would make a nice pendant. Carefully the goddess put it into a pocket.

She then stepped to the statue and examined it, the slender nymph figure hiding behind a tree gazing at...well, nothing now. Originally the piece had been paired with the statue of Narcissus, staring at his own reflection.

The sculptor who'd created these pieces had been a genius, helped out by a little influence from her. Both statues had held magic. Narcissus's statue had come to life and Echo's spirit had found the strength to become solid, leaving behind her stone home.

Both had found their true loves. Now Echo's former haunt was just a statue once more, beautiful even without her spirit inhabiting it. It was now just a work of art to be appreciated by many. She waved her hand and sent it back to the museum.

From the bower came a low-pitched, passion-filled cry. Aphrodite smiled in amusement. This pair was going to be a handful, she could tell. When should she tell them the truth about the arrow? Not now, that was for sure.

The goddess chuckled softly. "See Pan, I did get the last laugh."

She twirled the bow like a cheerleader's baton and flicked her fingers once more. Moments later another cry came from the bower, but there was no one in the garden to hear it anymore.

Epilogue

Unaccountably anxious, Alex waited outside the kitchen of the Mythology Inn. The newest restaurant in town, it had become a major success during the past six months, attracting the folks from the university as well as the local townsfolk with its mixture of old Grecian recipes and wide range of prices.

It was said that anyone, even the poorest student could afford a good meal at the Mythology Inn.

The restaurant was Chloe's brainchild. She'd used her cooking and organizational skills to attract the backers. Now that it was a success, there was talk of creating a franchise out of it and opening branches in other cities.

That was one of the reasons he was nervous. The other had to do with the letters he needed to show her, and a question he needed to ask.

It was well after midnight. The kitchen staff would be going home soon.

It still seemed odd not to be going to work at this time of night. He'd quit his job at the museum, instead doing the odd portrait work to bring some money in. Not as much money, but he could stay in bed with Chloe after they made love.

Between the two of them they were doing okay. Well, actually, they were doing better than okay, and it was time he did something to make sure things stayed that way.

The kitchen door opened and men and women filed out, tired but happy, looking forward to going home to the special people who shared their lives. They smiled and nodded at Alex, knowing whom it was he waited outside the door for.

When the last of them were gone, he slipped into the kitchen.

Her long hair pinned up in a neat bun, Chloe sat at one of the counters, still doing paperwork. She glanced up when he walked in and smiled warmly, a touch of surprise in her face. "I didn't expect to see you here."

"I couldn't wait to talk to you. Something happened today."

"Oh?" Her gaze took in the letters in his hand and her eyes widened. "You heard from the big studios you applied to," she guessed.

Alex grinned at her, and grabbed a seat next to her. "I certainly did. Have a look." He passed her the papers and watched as she read each carefully.

"Oh, Alex, this is wonderful. New York, San Francisco, Chicago. They all want you."

"That they do. And that causes a problem. Now I have to pick which offer to accept and for that I need your help."

Chloe looked up at him with those beautiful green eyes of hers. "Why do you need my help, Alex?"

He leaned forward onto the counter. "Because I need to know where the investors want to put the new Mythology Inn."

She caught her breath. "They were talking about San Francisco."

"Then that's the offer I'll take. That way we can move together." He grinned at her. "You didn't think I was going to let you get away from me, did you?"

Chloe threw her arms around his neck. "Oh Alex, that's so wonderful."

"Hey, babe, it's all right." He stroked her back and lifted her chin. Her eyes were bright with unshed tears. "No crying. You remember what I said."

She dashed them away with her hand. "Yeah, I know. I don't cry well."

"No you don't, so I need to keep you happy. Hmm, I wonder what would make you happy right now."

Laughter bubbled out of her. "Oh, I don't know. What would you suggest?"

He grinned at her. "You remember that night we first met in the museum?"

She blushed furiously. "You mean when I sneaked out of my statue and watched Nick and Violet making love?"

"That's it." He toyed with her blouse, pulling it out of the waistband of her skirt reaching around to stroke the soft skin underneath. "Ever since that night, I've had a wild desire to make love to a woman on her own desk." Alex glanced over at the office door in the corner of the kitchen. "Why, I believe there is a desk in there."

Chloe giggled as he hoisted her into his arms and carried her into the office, placing her on the edge of the desk. He pulled her skirt up, revealing the sweet little panties she'd worn that day. Bright pink, and he bet she had the matching bra on. Slowly Chloe undid her blouse, one button at a time.

Alex grinned as soon as he saw the pink bra. He'd won his bet.

He undid the fastening at the front and the bra split open, spilling her breasts into his hands. Nice, maybe even nicer than when they'd first met. She'd gained some weight and a lot of it had gone here, into these beautiful globes. Alex leaned in to taste the nipples, first one then the other.

They might have gotten bigger, but her breasts tasted the same. Still Chloe-flavored with plump nipples that he loved to hold between his lips. He indulged himself, sucking on her breast, pulling the tender tips with his teeth, while Chloe's hands tangled in his hair.

"Chloe, you taste like dessert, you're so sweet."

She giggled. "Really? You want dessert?" With a mischievous grin she hopped off the desk and headed for the kitchen. Alex waited, wondering what she was up to, until she returned carrying a familiar metal can with a nozzle top.

She brandished it. "Maybe you'd like a little whipped topping then."

Ah, that was Chloe, always appealing to his sweet tooth. Grinning, Alex grabbed the can and squirted a little of the white creamy foam across her lips. He bent to lick it off at the same time she tried to taste it, and their tongues tangled. Their lips merged into a creamy mess that required two tongues to clean up. Both were laughing by the time the last of the cream was gone from their faces.

Alex brandished the can. "Let's see what other parts go well with whipped cream."

Moment's later Chloe's underwear was on the floor and her pussy was covered in sweet foam. Alex stuck a finger in and licked it. "Chloe, you look tasty. Good enough to eat."

"So eat me, Alex."

Alex diligently set to work removing the cream with his tongue, eliciting first giggles then long moans from her. So sweet, even when the cream was gone, and her own flavors took over. Chloe was the tastiest woman he'd ever known.

Inside his pants his cock grew rock-hard and needy. He'd bust a zipper if he didn't get it out of there soon. Alex fumbled to free himself until Chloe's hands took over, carefully easing him out of his pants.

Holding his cock in her hand, she grabbed the can and sprayed a little on the tip. Alex jerked as the cold topping hit his over-sensitized penis.

Chloe giggled. "Now, now, I didn't complain. Don't worry, I'll warm it up." Her lips closed over his cock, drawing him deep inside her mouth.

Shit, fuck, damn that was good! After experiencing the cold whipped cream, her mouth felt so hot on his cock. So good, so very, very good. Great even.

Too great. "Chloe, stop, I'm going to come."

She pulled him out of her mouth and grinned up at him. "Well, we can't have that, can we?"

No one ever teased him the way she did. "On your hands and knees, woman. I want to fuck you now."

Shaking with suppressed laughter, Chloe followed his instructions, her beautiful ass facing him. Alex spread her cheeks, searching for the opening to her pussy. He needed to fuck her, hard, then soft, then however she wanted it, but he needed to fuck her right now. He placed his cock at the entry to her pussy and slid a little in her, moving her hips toward him. Then he pulled back and thrust deep inside.

Chloe moaned, her giggles gone. She rocked forward and back on her hands and knees, keeping with his rhythm, using the push and pull of Alex's hands to guide her movements.

Not that she needed guidance, any more than he did. They'd been lovers too long now to not know each other's needs, wants, and what it took to give happiness. Most of the time for Alex, all it took was one of Chloe's smiles.

At the moment, her rocking pussy was making him weak with pleasure. He drove in once, twice more, and felt her contract around him, her pussy squeezing tight around his cock, and she gasped out his name.

"Alex, oh *shit!*"

Alex gasped—Chloe never swore. Then she let out a scream, and he forgot about anything else as he drove deep within her, his seed spilling into her depths.

She collapsed under him, and he fell next to her on the floor. Dragging her into his arms, Alex nibbled the back of her neck.

"Mine," he said.

Her laugh was shaky. "Yes dear, all yours. Always, Alex."

He turned her onto her back and stared down at her. "Always, Chloe?"

"Yes, always."

Exaltation filled him. "All right. Prove it."

Chloe looked confused. "How should I do that?"

Grabbing at his pants, now gathered around his knees, Alex fetched the small box he'd hidden in his pocket. He handed it to her.

Opening it, she stared at the diamond ring. Not too big, but not too small. A little old-fashioned in style, but so was Chloe. "It was my grandmother's," he told her.

Chloe gazed up at him, her clothes undone, hair fallen from its bun, traces of whipped cream on her chin. She was a mess and he'd never seen her so beautiful.

"What do I say?" she asked, her voice a whisper.

"Say yes, please. I want our relationship legalized. Having Aphrodite's blessing is great, but if we're going to have those babies she was talking about, we need a marriage license."

"Babies?" Her eyes lit with joy and Alex knew he'd guessed right. Chloe did want children.

"Yeah, babe. Babies." He stroked her smooth stomach. "I'd love to take your picture with my kid inside."

"Love, Alex? That's not a safe word for you."

"It is where you're concerned." He put the ring on her finger. "I love you and I want you to be my wife. Is the answer yes?"

She smiled at him. "Yes, Alex. Yes to being your wife, yes to the babies. I love you, too."

He took her in his arms. "I think there's an echo in here." She giggled as he licked the last of the whipped cream off her chin. "I love you, babe."

Enjoy this excerpt from:
TWO MEN AND A LADY
LADY'S CHOICE

© Copyright Cricket Starr

Funny, she'd never really been interested in two men at the same time, but both these guys made her mouth water. More than her mouth, actually. The crotch of her spacer suit dampened with her arousal and she crossed her legs, hoping they wouldn't notice.

Both men's gaze riveted below her belt and they sniffed the air, their eyes glazing for a moment. Her eyes widened at their reaction. *Oh, yeah, they'd noticed.* They must have superb senses of smell.

The front of both men's trousers tightened into a pair of impressive packages. In the back of her mind, Lija took in their sizes and did the math. Yep, either of them would do nicely for her last fling of freedom before buckling under to her fate.

Too bad she only needed one. Choosing was going to be tough.

She waved her hand at the chairs next to her at the round table. "Would you gentlemen like to sit down?"

The pair exchanged nearly angry looks as they took their positions, one on each side of her. The redheaded man carrying the mugs slammed them down on the table hard enough to spill some of the contents.

His companion glared at him. "I don't need your help."

"I'm not offering help. You forgot your drink."

"I didn't need a drink, either."

Lija put up her hands. "Gentlemen, please. Here I was feeling lonely and now I have two lovely men to keep me company." She waved to the bartender. "Please, a pitcher for my new friends."

Both men had their credit chips out. "You won't be paying," the blond one told her.

"I'll buy," the redhead said at the same time.

Blue eyes narrowed into slits. "No, I'll buy."

"Not on your life."

"Don't tempt me."

The pair glared at each other then both men's right fists came up.

"Now just a zeminute..." she said, wishing to stop the fight, but to her surprise they chanted in unison, pounding their fists on the table.

"Ti, To, Te."

Red's fist had one finger sticking out, Blondie's had turned into an open palm.

"Sword slices Ax. I win," the red-haired man said smugly.

Blondie glared and folded his arms, but allowed his buddy to pass over the credit chips for the pitcher.

Lija smiled. These hulking he-men played a children's game to settle disputes? *This was going to be fun.* "So, may I ask my companions for their names?"

Red spoke first. "I'm Gehon Avermoe. This is my friend, Jackon Overton."

She extended her hand. "My name is Lija. And I'm pleased to meet you."

Jackon's hand slashed out first, barely beating Gehon's. His palm covered hers possessively. "Not nearly as pleased as I am to meet you, my lady." Pulling her hand to his lips, he kissed it gently. His lips tingled the back of her hand and between her legs the dampness grew.

Lija gulped. At this rate she'd soon need padded undergarments.

Gehon captured her other hand and pulled it to his lips. "I cannot speak of how wonderful it is to meet you, Lady Lija."

Caught between the two of them nibbling her hands, Lija wondered that she was able to breathe. Hot and cold flushes ran up and down her spine, pooling in her dampened groin.

She seriously needed one of these men to bed her. Trouble was, which one? What a delicious dilemma for one woman to have.

Jackon's blue eyes glared over her hand at his friend. "Her taste is for me, Gehon."

Brown eyes narrowed into a matching glare. "Her taste is mine, Jackon."

They stared at each other, then suddenly both men sat up, eyes widening and jaws dropping in unison. Gehon licked the back of the hand he held, Jackon doing the same with his. Lija shivered under their tongues.

"What do you taste?" the redhead asked.

The blond licked his lips relishing the flavor there. "Sweet. Like honeybeets."

"Sweeter than that. Caramallow."

"Mellowdrops."

"Chocoberries."

They both dropped her hands and Lija pulled them back to her side of the table as the men stared at each other, and then at her.

"The same for both of us?" Jackon said, his voice heavy with disbelief.

"So it seems. A cosmic joke," Gehon replied.

About the author:

Cricket Starr lives in the San Francisco Bay area with her husband of more years than she chooses to count. She loves fantasies, particularly sexual fantasies, and sees her writing as an opportunity to test boundaries. Her driving ambition is to have more fun than anyone should or could have. While published in other venues under her own name, she's found a home for her erotica writing here at Ellora's Cave.

Cricket welcomes mail from readers. You can write to her c/o Ellora's Cave Publishing at 1337 Commerce Drive, Suite 13, Stow OH 44224.

Why an electronic book?

We live in the Information Age—an exciting time in the history of human civilization in which technology rules supreme and continues to progress in leaps and bounds every minute of every hour of every day. For a multitude of reasons, more and more avid literary fans are opting to purchase e-books instead of paperbacks. The question to those not yet initiated to the world of electronic reading is simply: *why?*

1. *Price.* An electronic title at Ellora's Cave Publishing runs anywhere from 40-75% less than the cover price of the <u>exact same title</u> in paperback format. Why? Cold mathematics. It is less expensive to publish an e-book than it is to publish a paperback, so the savings are passed along to the consumer.

2. *Space.* Running out of room to house your paperback books? That is one worry you will never have with electronic novels. For a low one-time cost, you can purchase a handheld computer designed specifically for e-reading purposes. Many e-readers are larger than the average handheld, giving you plenty of screen room. Better yet, hundreds of titles can be stored within your new library—a single microchip. (Please note that Ellora's Cave does not endorse any specific brands. You can check our website at www.ellorascave.com for customer

recommendations we make available to new consumers.)

3. *Mobility.* Because your new library now consists of only a microchip, your entire cache of books can be taken with you wherever you go.

4. *Personal preferences are accounted for.* Are the words you are currently reading too small? Too large? Too…**ANNOYING**? Paperback books cannot be modified according to personal preferences, but e-books can.

5. *Innovation.* The way you read a book is not the only advancement the Information Age has gifted the literary community with. There is also the factor of what you can read. Ellora's Cave Publishing will be introducing a new line of interactive titles that are available in e-book format only.

6. *Instant gratification.* Is it the middle of the night and all the bookstores are closed? Are you tired of waiting days—sometimes weeks—for online and offline bookstores to ship the novels you bought? Ellora's Cave Publishing sells instantaneous downloads 24 hours a day, 7 days a week, 365 days a year. Our e-book delivery system is 100% automated, meaning your order is filled as soon as you pay for it.

Those are a few of the top reasons why electronic novels are displacing paperbacks for many an avid reader. As always, Ellora's Cave Publishing welcomes your questions and comments. We invite you to email us at service@ellorascave.com or write to us directly at: 1337 Commerce Drive, Suite 13, Stow OH 44224.

Discover for yourself why readers can't get enough of the multiple award-winning publisher Ellora's Cave. Whether you prefer e-books or paperbacks, be sure to visit EC on the web at www.ellorascave.com for an erotic reading experience that will leave you breathless.

WWW.ELLORASCAVE.COM

Printed in the United States
25496LVS00005B/304-417